BOOK TWO OF THE VAMPIRE WAR

NIGHT FURY

CHRONICLES OF THE OTHERWORLD

MELISSA CUMMINS

Cover by Melissa Cummins

Editing and Proofreading by E.M Editing

Formatting by Melissa Cummins

Published by Melissa Cummins on June 14th, 2022

ISBN: 978-1958769997

ALSO BY MELISSA CUMMINS

CHRONICLES OF THE OTHERWORLD

Part 1. The Vampire War

Dark Vampire and Witch Romance (Interconnected Standalones best read in this order)

Night Shade

Night Fury

Night Fall

Part 2. Feral Wolves - Coming Soon

Dark Omegaverse/Shifter Romance (Standalones read in any order)

Carnal Claim - Coming Soon

Bitten To Obey - Coming Soon

Primal Hunger - Coming Soon

Savage Embrace - Coming Soon

Part 3. Fae - Coming Soon

Dark Fae Romance (Standalones best read in any order)

Fae Book 1 - Coming Soon

Fae Book 2 - Coming Soon

Fae Book 3 - Coming Soon

STANDALONES

My Brutal Beast

Crowned In Blood

My Vicious Beast - Coming Soon

DEDICATION

To those who have been hurt. To those who have been wronged. To those who may have believed the world left you to rot. You have a home out there, someone who loves and supports you.
Don't give up, even when it's hard. Don't give up.

NEVER MISS A RELEASE

To get information on works in progress, new releases, and receive exclusive discounts, giveaways, and bonus content, make sure to subscribe to my newsletter!

AUTHOR'S NOTE

Believe it or not, this book is what made me decide to start publishing the Chronicles of The Otherworld series. It's deep, disturbing, hard, and gritty. The love story is beautiful, but what both of these characters have been through isn't. If you like love that preservers through every obstacle and characters that refuse to give up on one another, this book is for you!

Night Fury is the second in the Chronicles of The Otherworld series, as well as the second book in part one, The Vampire War. Each part of the series will feature a different paranormal species. Each book will feature a different couple and will always have a Happy Ever After (HEA) for that couple.

While I always recommend reading from beginning of the series for the best experience, Night Fury is an inter-connected standalone which continues on from the plot of Night Shade.

The tropes are: Strong, Scarred, Tortured, Curvy, Human Witch, Billionaire, Protective Vampire Hero, Fated Mates, Angst, Kidnapped, Not good enough, Amnesia, Morally Gray Couple, Touch Her/Him and Die Vibes, and I'll Never Let You Go.

Night Fury is intended for mature audiences. This story contains mentions and detailed depictions of physical, emotional, mental, and sexual abuse, including rape and sexual harassment, suicidal thoughts, extreme violence, murder, death, torture, explicit language, sexually explicit scenes, and blood drinking.

This book also heavily discusses negative self-talk, feelings of unworthiness and inadequacy, criticism, depression, PTSD, manipulation, trauma, amnesia, and therapy.

The following kinks have also been included in this work: agoraphilia, begging, breeding, praise, primal, Dom and Brat behavior, breath play, and spanking.

Reader discretion is advised.

PLAYLIST

Want to listen along while you read? Search CoTO: Night Fury on Spotify or scan the QR code below:

Bring Me To Life - Evanescence
Feel Good - Gryffin, ILLENIUM, feat. Daya
A Little More - Alessia Cara
One Night - Christina Perri
Light Me Up - RL Grime, Miguel, Julia Michaels
Not Giving In - Tom Walker
Waking Up - MJ Cole, Freya Ridings
Mind Is A Prison - Alec Benjamin
Artistry - Jacob Lee
Good Enough - Evanescence
Courage To Change - Sia
Hollow - Submersed
Distance - Yebba
Shadows - Canyon City

CHAPTER 1

THE DAY OF THE BATTLE

Something called to Luke, playing with the fringes of his mind, teasing him with answers to questions he'd never dared to speak out loud. But he needed those answers desperately. He needed them to help make sense of everything he'd felt over the last few months, and they were worth everything, even Greg's wrath.

Luke ran away from the group, ignoring Greg's shout. He followed the call as it pulled him further down the passage. It turned, narrowed, and then opened to a full room. The moment Luke entered, he was forced to duck, missing a punch aimed at his head.

"You weren't who I was hoping for." Zachariah smirked, his brown eyes gleaming. "But you'll do."

Luke rushed him. He landed a punch to Zachariah's face and another to his gut before jumping back in time to miss Zachariah's counterattack. Ducking under a kick, Luke delivered a punch to the underside of Zachariah's knee, satisfied when the bone splintered.

It wasn't enough.

Zachariah caught him with an elbow to the chest. He kneed Luke in his ribs before punching the side of his head. When Zachariah's kick connected, Luke flew back, rolling until he hit the cavern wall.

Luke stood slowly, faking weakness. The healing agent in his blood was already working through his system and renewing his strength, but he needed to be smart about this. Zachariah's enhanced strength would make him difficult to take down directly, and there was still speculation that Zachariah could copy another immortal's ability. Without knowing how that ability worked, being impulsive could land Luke in a very dangerous situation.

And then there was Johanna. She stood in the middle of the room, her face blank, emotionless. She was still under Zachariah's control. Luke had strategically pulled Zachariah away from Johanna during the fight, but he was still too close to her. Luke knew that if pushed, Zachariah would use Johanna as a hostage, and Luke would never risk her life. The best strategy was to tire Zachariah out without using his abilities. If Luke made him believe that he was weaker, Zachariah would grow cocky, ensuring Luke's victory.

As Luke went to step forward, his body froze. An unseen pressure knocked him to his knees. He struggled against it, but the bone-crushing weight held him down, pushing his stomach flat against the dirt.

"*Luke?*" a soft voice whispered in his head.

His eyes darted around the room, but no one else had entered. Zachariah stood unmoving, entirely too still, and Luke wondered if he felt the same pressure. Luke's eyes darted to Johanna. While she hadn't moved, something seemed different about her—electric.

Confused, he responded mentally, "*Johanna?*"

"*Good.*" Her sigh of relief flitted through him. "*You can hear me.*"

"*How are you doing this? What are you—*"

"*That doesn't matter now. Please, stay down and lie still. Don't fight me.*"

Something akin to panic squeezed at his chest. Was it hers or was it his? "*Johanna, whatever this is, stop it. Let me go.*"

"*No!*" The force of her shout was so strong it made his ears ring. "*You don't understand. You can't kill him!*"

"*Yes, I can!*" Luke tried to will his body to move but it wasn't responding to him.

"*No, you can't!*" Johanna's voice softened. "*Please, stop. Zachariah isn't the leader you've believed him to be. It's someone else, and she is far more powerful than you or I. If you kill him, she will come after you, and she won't stop until she breaks you. I don't ... I don't want to see you hurt. I don't want anyone to ever experience that again. Now please, stop—*"

"*Johanna—*"

"We don't have any more time! You'll be able to move when I'm gone. As soon as you can, take the passage to the left. It'll lead you outside."

Zachariah suddenly twitched and shook his head, as if coming out of a daze. He stared down at Luke and then *tsked*. "I thought he would have lasted longer. Oh well." He turned toward Johanna. "Since he left me so unsatisfied, you'll have to make up for it. Now, let's go." Zachariah grabbed her by the arm and dragged her behind him.

Johanna followed him meekly, but Luke heard her quiet sob in his mind, and recognition pierced his heart. He fought against the pressure holding him down like a wild man.

Move! Move damn it! Move! he urged himself.

"I'm sorry," she hiccuped. *"At least you'll be safe. Goodbye, Luke."*

"Johanna!" he screamed, fighting against her power until she disappeared around a corridor.

And just like that, she was gone.

———

Luke was still screaming when he woke up.

Every night for the last two months Luke had awoken drenched in sweat, his mouth open, screaming at the horrible memory. It never changed, never stopped, never got better, never distorted. It was always the same. It was the day he finally got the answer to one of his questions, the moment he realized Johanna was his mate.

The four walls of his bedroom felt like they were closing in, and the air was too hot, too humid to breathe. He kicked off the covers and goosebumps raced over his skin as a brush of cool air flitted over him. He was the problem—not this room, not this house, not anything else. He was the one who was broken, the one who had failed.

He'd failed Johanna. Occasionally, Luke would relive his nightmare as a specter. His corporal form would float just above the unfolding scene, and in those moments he'd revisit everything. If he had taken more risks instead of being concerned about Zachariah stealing his power, if he had moved closer to Johanna instead of away, would she have felt safe enough to reach out to him then? Would she be in his arms right now?

Those weren't the only times he should have fought harder for her. Luke would give anything to go back to the times he'd tried to speak to Johanna at work and she'd run away from him. If he had followed her, pressed her to explain why she kept avoiding him, would she be here right now? If nothing else, he would have finally known why she was able to combat the connection between them, the mate bond that had finally snapped into place in that cavern.

Luke would even have been at peace if she had outright rejected him. It would have devastated and destroyed him, but this? Not knowing if she was even … He couldn't go there, not again, because if she wasn't alive, he'd lose it. He'd lose every single piece of himself and spend the last remaining minutes of his life killing Zachariah and anyone else he could get his hands on before they took him down.

The only thing that gave him hope was that after being on the receiving end of Johanna's powers, he knew Zachariah would never give her up easily. She was extraordinarily powerful. A feeling of pride for his mate flashed through his heart before it was crushed under the heavy weight of despair. If it weren't for those powers, would she even be in that position?

No, she'd be dead.

That thought had him reaching out before his arm froze in mid-air, shaking so badly with the need to hurt, to break, to destroy with his rage. Luke took a deep breath, then another, and another, trying to settle his mind.

The simple fact was that if Johanna wasn't powerful and Zachariah discovered she was Luke's mate, he would have killed her, much like he had tried to kill Daniella. At least this way Johanna was alive, and Luke was sure she would stay that way.

But that still didn't answer how Johanna had hidden their mate bond, and Luke was sure she had. Even if she were able to hide it from everyone else, he should have been able to feel it immediately. And why was it that he finally felt their mate bond in that cavern when she had seemed so ... different? So real? When her voice seemed softer yet stronger than he had ever heard it, and she had become so determined, so protective over him? Why then and not before?

Luke rested his head back against the headboard and ran a shaky hand through his brown hair, swiping the stuck strands from his forehead. No matter how hard he tried to figure it out, he couldn't. Every time one mystery resolved itself, another one unfurled. It was endless, and it would stay that way until he found her—and he *would* find her. But rage still barred its fangs and tore at him, peeling back more and more layers until it reached his soul and covered it in something dark and sadistic.

Luke sighed. He couldn't keep doing this. He couldn't keep being this way. It wouldn't be good for the battle tonight, yet another attempt at finding her.

You'll find her. You'll find her, he chanted in his head, hoping that thinking the words would somehow make them come true.

Luke needed to move, to do something to keep his mind busy. Checking his phone, he saw he'd only slept for two hours and had another two before he'd have to drive to Greg and Daniella's home for the strategy meeting. He cracked his knuckles and left his room, heading toward his gym where he beat and kicked the punching bag, unleashing a fraction of his wrath until the bag itself exploded. But even then he didn't stop, not until he'd ripped it to shreds.

CHAPTER 2

The wind picked up, tousling Luke's hair as he sped down the back roads to Greg and Daniella's house. He'd be a little early for the strategy meeting, but he needed the escape.

Breaking that punching bag felt good, too good, and he would have moved on to something else if he'd stayed home. His emotions had always been a little too intense—passionate was the word Luke liked to use— but while he was known for being a loose cannon, for the first time in his life he felt like one.

Luke took another deep breath, like Dani kept telling him he should do, and let the fresh air carry away his thoughts. He wasn't alone here, even if he felt like it in his rage and anguish. He was surrounded by people who loved him, people who were willing to fight to help him get Johanna back. And even though that was more than most could ask for, it wasn't enough. It would never be enough, not until she was by his side.

Luke's somber mood engulfed him as he approached the house. He swiped his badge and froze at the entrance when he heard Dani laugh, knowing he'd intruded on something. The sound was cut short, and Luke sighed before shutting the door.

Greg and Daniella were sympathetic to Luke's grief and tried not to do anything that would remind him of his pain, including being affectionate in front of him. It hurt Luke to be grateful for that. He wanted them to be happy and had always pushed for them to be together, but if he was being honest, he couldn't stand seeing it now. And for that, he was a bastard. He loathed and cursed the part of him that couldn't witness two people he loved be happy, not when he knew that his person wasn't next to him.

But she will be, he reminded himself again.

As he entered the kitchen, Dani greeted him with a soft smile and met him for a hug. "Hey, you."

"Hey," Luke said as he feigned a small smile, but she was on to him. Dani squeezed his arm as they separated and her dark brown eyes met his, full of concern, worry, and something else.

Luke averted his gaze, not wanting her to see how close he was to drowning in the weight of his emotions, and instead looked over her head to Greg. "Sorry I'm a little early."

"No, you're actually right on time," Greg said, exchanging a hug with Luke next.

Confused, Luke moved to join them at the breakfast nook, taking a seat on the barstool across from them. "Is something going on?"

Dani gave him a tiny smile, her voice soft as she passed him a manilla folder. "You should know before everyone else. I hope ... I hope it helps."

Luke looked between her and Greg, but their faces gave nothing away. Suddenly the folder seemed too heavy, as if it held the weight of his damnation, salvation, or both. Fear swam through Luke's veins. He was terrified that if he opened the envelope, the small bit of hope he held onto would be ruined, that the ground would break open under him to swallow him whole.

"Go on, open it." Dani squeezed his hand. "It's okay."

Luke looked at the comparison of their skin on top of one another—Dani's dark brown, to his olive—and used it as a visual aid, an anchor to remind him that she and Greg were right there. He would not drown. They would keep him afloat.

With more care than Luke had ever taken with anything in his whole life, he opened the folder. In it was a pack of pages with faces of people who worked for their company. Luke tilted his head as he recognized the data from their HRIS system, and then he saw it. An extra number on the first page circled, another on the next, two on the next, five after that. Every page he flipped through had a circled set of numbers.

"I don't understand. What is this?" Luke asked, squeezing the folder too tight as his nerves began to furrow and bundle under his skin, making his heart beat faster.

"It will make sense with this." Greg handed him another folder, his hazel eyes gleaming.

Luke snatched it from him. Opening the folder, he first saw a header containing a key with numbers and corresponding page counts, which seemed familiar though out of place, and several sets of coordinates. On the other side were pictures of mapped areas.

The question of the key picked at Luke's mind, and he studied it until he realized what it meant. His eyes darted from one folder to another, comparing the numbers and flipping through the mapped areas and overview points of each location. The pieces fell together like that of a giant puzzle, and he realized that the key referenced the HRIS data folder, and the coordinates were made from the circled numbers within it. Luke finally looked up at Greg and Dani, and jabbed a finger at the paperwork. "Where did these come from? What's here?"

Greg slid his arm around Daniella's waist as he leaned forward to tap on the first set of coordinates. "This is where we're going today."

"And as for where we got them from"—Dani's eyes

shone as they stared into his own—"they came from Johanna."

"What?" Luke gasped, drawing back. "That's impossible, she's not ... We didn't—"

Find her, he finished internally, unable to say the words aloud.

"I asked Mya to look into what Johanna was doing before she was taken," Greg began.

Luke's throat constricted at the word 'taken,' and his shoulders tensed. Dani squeezed his hand again and he gave her a small nod, trying to convince them both that he was okay.

Greg tapped on one of the circled numbers. "Mya noticed that some of the employees' ID numbers were too long, some by one number, others by several." Greg tapped on the roster of locations next. "Once she figured out their pattern, Mya made the key and put together whatever coordinates she could. She was able to find seventeen locations. There's more to work through, but Mya can't make sense of them until we find Johanna."

Luke shook. He didn't know whether it was from excitement, hope or fear, but it was uncontrollable. It was only when Dani gave his hand another hard squeeze that his gaze flickered to hers and he realized he hadn't been breathing.

Breathe. You can't have a panic attack. You need to pay attention to what's going on here.

"It's okay," Dani said, as if she were reading his mind. "Just breathe, it's okay."

Luke nodded like a child and followed her advice: One breath, in, hold, out, second breath, in, hold, out, and another, and another.

Greg leaned forward, and Luke's wide eyes moved to his. Greg's presence reminded him that he was safe, that if Greg was in control, Luke could also be in control. Luke nodded again, and then once more, not trusting himself to speak.

"Luke, you know that I am going to do everything in my power to get her back to you, don't you?" Greg said.

Luke nodded again. He felt calmer, surer, and yet somehow still as if he were floating, as if he'd taken some sort of drug, maybe speed and acid mixed together, that had him flying through the clouds with a sputtering engine, constantly high but scared of the drop he knew would come.

"And you know that I wouldn't lie to you, right?" Greg said, his voice calm but strong.

Luke's hand balled into a tight fist under Dani's, and he watched as her gaze slid to Greg's and then back to his own. That drop, the free fall, the flipping of his stomach as gravity pulled him down, it was coming so fast, so soon, he could taste it. Still, Luke answered, "Yes."

Greg gave a short, stiff nod and then sighed. "We don't have any way to survey these areas before we attack them."

Luke understood immediately. They had no way to

confirm if Johanna was there, if his mate would be found in this location or any of the ones on this roster.

Greg continued. "We're going to hit them hard and fast. But by doing this we're running a risk. If Johanna is at any of these locations, we'll grab her, but if she isn't then they might move her ... or worse."

Blame her.

Luke swallowed. As far as they knew, she was the only one who had come into contact with the inner workings of both their group and Zachariah's. It would be easy for Zachariah to suspect her of slipping them information at some point, especially if they didn't find more information at the location they planned to raid in a few short hours.

"What's important to remember," Dani said, snapping Luke out of his thoughts, "is that somehow she found out about these locations. She could have found them on a computer or some sort of paperwork, but I don't think that's the case. There's simply too many for someone to remember unless they saw them several times."

"Or had been at those locations multiple times," Luke said.

"Exactly." Greg smiled. "And if she's been at these locations multiple times—"

"Then we might find her there." Luke breathed out heavily. The tightness in his chest floated out, and with it his eyes watered. He didn't even know tears had begun to slide down his cheeks until a droplet fell on the folder, quickly followed by another.

"We will find her," Greg said, his voice stern and sure. "There's plenty to worry about, Luke, but of that I can assure you."

"Th-thank you." Luke's voice cracked before he fully dissolved into tears, and his family wrapped him in their arms.

———

Luke took his seat at the table next to his cousin, Mya. They exchanged a small smile before he said, "Thank you."

Something in her eyes flickered, her face falling into a sad sort of kindness that echoed his own pain. Luke's heart broke for her. She was trying to help him fix his pain, when hers would never be resolved. Her mate, Erik, was dead.

"I'll always do anything I can to help you, you know that," Mya said.

Greg and Daniella entered the room, cutting their conversation short. Greg sat first, Daniella perching on the arm of the chair, as had become a custom for them. For the first time, Luke imagined Johanna there with him, her blonde hair flowing over her shoulders and down to her waist, her blue eyes scanning the room, studying everyone. He knew she'd be welcomed here, and not just because he was family and original to this circle. No, she would be welcomed because of the information Greg and Daniella had shared in the kitchen. In the history of their circle, no one had ever provided such important information about an enemy, and no one had ever risked their life to do so. When Luke found Johanna, he'd make sure to share with her exactly what he thought about her little contribution.

Mya kicked his leg under the table, calling attention to its restless bouncing. He immediately stopped, turning back to Greg and Daniella.

"We'll attack this location at 10:00 a.m., then these three locations at 3:00 p.m.," Greg said, using his pointer to identify each set of coordinates. "For the half of you that are here, we work like normal, three teams leaving in fifteen-minute increments to scope the location before we attack. However, when we return we will not have another strategy meeting. Instead, we will assign A, B, and C teams and hit the three locations at the same time. I will be in charge of team A. We've handpicked a team for Luke who will be in charge of team B—"

Luke blinked, his eyes widening at the statement. Never had Greg given him such a level of responsibility. Luke's abilities were best in sneak attacks, but he never expected to be trusted to fight on his own away from Greg and Mya. He was impulsive, quick to anger, and his patience only lasted for as long as he had to use it to outsmart his enemy.

Luke's mouth fell open, words coming to the

surface, but it closed when he caught the look in Dani's gaze, a simple smile that spoke volumes to him. *We trust you.*

Mya said something beside him, answered some question, and Luke snapped back to the present.

Greg gave her a single nod before turning back to the other members at the table. "We leave in fifteen."

CHAPTER 3

Luke met with his team.

Merida and Dominick were both people Luke admired and trusted. They understood his predicament; they were mated, and if there was anyone who could understand almost losing their mate and the trials to get them back, it was the two of them. Jason, Cara, and Anna completed their group, and he knew that their fighting styles and combined abilities strengthened an already incredible lineup that Luke couldn't believe he'd been assigned to lead. Yet not a single member looked at him the way he expected them to, as someone who wouldn't be able to guide them, whose irresponsibility would get them killed. Instead, they treated him with respect. Something about it made him feel proud, until the walls caved in and he realized this must be some sort of big mistake.

Luke excused himself and went to find Greg. He

needed to tell him this was wrong, that Greg should not entrust him with the lives of others. After all, look how well that had gone for Johanna.

He spotted Greg with his arm wrapped around Daniella, speaking to another battle officer. Dani caught his approach and a mischievous look crossed her face. Then she tilted her head up and whispered something into Greg's ear, causing him to turn to look at Luke as well.

Dani approached Luke, giving him a light pat on the shoulder. "Just accept it," she whispered before she sauntered away.

Luke blinked for a moment and then glared daggers into the back of her head. He knew she could feel his stare, just like she knew why he'd come to speak to Greg. Dani was his best friend, and she understood him in a way most people didn't. It also meant she was well versed on calling him out on his bullshit before he'd even opened his mouth, and she enjoyed doing it on a regular basis. But this wasn't about him, not really. It wasn't about pride, confidence, or his lack thereof. This was about the others and how they deserved someone who would lead them. Someone who could be cautious, level-headed, and would not snap at a moment's notice. Someone who was not him.

Luke followed Greg into another room, all the while grinding his teeth at Greg's nonchalance. He barely waited for the door to close before he started.

"What the hell were you thinking?" Luke shouted.

"I'm not fit to run a team. I'm not reliable or responsible enough for this, and those people, *your* people, are going to be at risk!"

Greg cocked an eyebrow, his tone even as he spoke. "What are you talking about, Luke?"

"You know exactly what I'm talking about." Luke huffed, burning a path into the carpet as he paced. "Greg, I'm not a leader like you are. Do I need to remind you that I ran off on not just you, someone who has practically raised me, but Mya, Dani, and the rest of your team, just because I thought I could rescue my mate? And I couldn't even do that right. I even had Zachariah in the palm of my hand!" Luke hands balled into fists as he shook them. "I wasn't able to kill him, and you think it's a smart idea to have me lead a team?"

"Luke—" Greg began, but Luke interrupted him, his shoulders drooping as he went on.

"Greg, let's just cut to the chase and be honest here. There's a reason why people think of me the way they do, and they're not wrong. I shouldn't be trusted with other people's lives. If we weren't related, I wouldn't even be this high in the circle. I've already failed enough for one lifetime, so please don't make me ruin someone else's life just because you're trying to be supportive or give me a distraction. This isn't the right way."

"Lucas," Greg bit out, his tone laced with anger. "Has anyone ever said any of those things to you?"

Luke rolled his eyes. "Of course not, but—"

"Then why the fuck are you saying them?" Greg shouted.

"Because they're the truth!" Luke shouted back. "And you know they are too!"

Greg tensed. "The only negative things I've ever called you are crazy and a pain in my ass."

"Greg—"

"Let me finish."

Luke ground his teeth but kept silent.

"Do you know what circle members have to agree to before we allow them to become battle officers?"

"No." Luke crossed his arms, narrowing his eyes. "It's another one of the many things I don't know."

Greg glared at him but continued. "They agree to take direction and action from us, to acknowledge that we are capable of leading. If any of them, *any* of them, ever said those things to you or disrespected you in *any* way, they wouldn't have a seat at our table."

Luke's eyes widened. "But—"

"Furthermore, every single person who joined your team volunteered."

"What?" Luke's mouth fell open.

"Yeah, they volunteered." Greg pushed a hand through his russet-colored hair. "Luke, have you always felt this way? That we … that I don't value you?"

Luke averted his gaze from Greg's form. "It's not that, I just … No, I don't think I felt that way before…"

"Johanna?"

Luke flinched at her name. "Yes. But still, I can be

honest enough to say I haven't always made the right decisions. I haven't lived my life the way you've lived yours, being cautious and responsible. I've lived to have fun, to enjoy life. Then we lost Erik, and everything was just numb." He smiled slightly. "Until Daniella."

Greg's lips tilted upward, just briefly. "Until Daniella."

"It was so good to see that you had found your mate, especially with it being such a rare thing for us, and with Dani and I being so close it made me feel better, like I had some sort of purpose. But then Johanna came into the picture and everything has been upside down for me ever since. I handled everything wrong, Greg, everything, and I guess it's just made me reflect on the other choices I've made in my life." It was Luke's turn to run a hand through his own brown hair, ruffling the strands, fraying them to match the state of his nerves.

Greg tapped the desk, then nodded to a chair. "Sit please, we need to work this out."

Luke obliged and waited for him to speak.

"You said you weren't like me, and that's true, you're not." Greg's eyes bore into Luke's own. "But you don't need to be. You're just you, and that's exactly who you should be. Yes, you've made brash decisions, but so have I. Yes, you can be more impulsive than I am, more impatient, and to some that makes you irresponsible."

Luke's gaze shifted away from Greg's as shame filled him.

"But," Greg said, his tone sharp enough to pull

Luke's attention back to him, "that doesn't mean you're less than anyone else here, including myself. The same people who would call you any of those things are the same people who may not like the decisions I make to keep this circle running. Do you really think everyone agrees with me all the time?"

Luke shook his head. "Of course not, but—"

"But *nothing*. If you can see that, then you should also be able to see that no one would believe you're any of those things all the time. Yes, you ran after Johanna on your own, but did you know we all wanted to run after you, to abandon everything and make sure you were safe? The only reason anyone hesitated was because they rely on me, and I had to force myself to walk away from you. I had to trust and believe you knew how to keep yourself safe, and if you needed help, the others would do right by you." Greg breathed. "Was I pissed? Of course, but not just at you. I was upset at myself for not being able to do what I wanted to, which was take care of my little cousin." He smiled.

If Luke had felt like himself, he would have rolled his eyes at the sentiment, but he didn't. Luke held onto Greg's words with a vice grip, finally understanding just how much he needed them. Luke had thought his heart had grown cold, surrounded by the ice he believed he needed to keep his distance from everyone else, because if that ice cracked, he would hurt everyone and they would see just how weak he had become. But the look on Greg's face, so soft, filled with a kindness that shone in his eyes and in his smile, made Luke realize that maybe the ice wasn't his ally. Maybe it was keeping him trapped instead of keeping him safe.

"Luke," Greg began, "I need you. I need you here and in the circle. You know me well enough to know I don't say that lightly. It hurts me to know I made you think you were replaceable or not enough, even for a moment."

Greg sighed. "I've always hated what happened during our childhood, so I wanted to take care of you. I didn't want you to ever feel alone again. But I pushed too hard." He slumped forward, clasping onto the desk with his palms to support his torso. "I wanted you to live your life as a child should, and then as a vampire should be able to. If you wanted money, women, fun, entertainment, whatever, I wanted you to have that. I wanted you to be able to enjoy your life with no attachments or responsibility, with nothing but support from me while not needing to concern yourself with me. That's the reason I haven't given you circle responsibilities, like Mya or Merida and Dom. But that doesn't mean I could ever replace you. You are irreplaceable to me."

Luke swallowed down the ball of emotions in his throat and watched as Greg did the same.

"You keep me honest, don't you know that? You're the only one who walks in here like he owns the place and has the balls to call me out. I trust you in that way. You argue with me, you fight with me to make sure I always do what's right. Luke, you're not only just as much of a part of this circle as I am, you run it with me. I may be the figurehead, the person who attends the meetings, puts things in place, and issues the orders, but it is not without your counsel."

Luke was breaking apart, physically and emotionally. He had to use his arms to support his head, as his elbows dug into his knees to keep from sliding to the ground.

How could I be so stupid? No, stop. You're doing it again. You are not stupid, you were just ... blind.

"I envy you sometimes," Greg whispered, making Luke's head snap up. "You don't know how many times I've had to stop my reactions and contain my emotions because the people around me needed me to be their sense of calm. But you don't have to do that. Why would I ever want to chain you down and reduce you to what I go through on a daily basis? Look at myself and Ella. Look how long we waited. Do you think I would ever want you to go through something like that? You even helped keep me sane with her."

Luke's eyes widened. "What are you talking about?"

"I trusted you to look out for her, Luke. That's why when I went out of town or overseas, I never asked anyone to look out for her. I knew you would. I trusted you with the safety of my mate. If nothing else can explain to you how I think of you, how much I value you, that should tell you everything."

Luke grasped the bridge of his nose and took a long, deep breath. "I can't ... I didn't even think of that."

"Well, now you are, so late is better than never." Greg smiled.

Luke glared at him before they chuckled, the laugh clearing the tension in the room. "I'm sorry for all of this. I guess ... I just didn't realize how much this had messed me up." He sighed. "I never stopped to see things from your perspective, and that was wrong of me."

"No, it was wrong of me to never tell you. We all have faults, right? I'm learning one of mine is that I tend to not share things. I would rather carry the burden alone so that it won't hurt others."

Luke chuckled. "Sounds like Dani is keeping you in line."

Greg laughed with him. "She's definitely trying. Listen, whatever it is you're going through now, however you're feeling, you need to know it's okay. Luke, you're worried about the safety of your mate. You're in despair and that will fuck with you in the absolute worst ways. In those moments, everything you do feels like it's not enough, like it's caving in and you can't breathe."

Luke breathed for a moment before he settled, and a little more of the ice around his heart cracked. "You're right, it does. I feel that way all the time. It makes me feel so ... useless, and then I just become so angry. Angry at myself, angry at everyone, the world, fate. Do you know how many things I've broken at my house? It's getting expensive."

Greg's eyebrow rose. "You have over a billion dollars in dividends from company stocks."

"And if we don't find Johanna soon, they'll be finished by the end of the week." He sighed. "It's pitiful. I've never felt so weak."

Greg nodded. "I've felt like that many times, especially recently."

Luke didn't need to ask. He knew what Greg was talking about. When Daniella had been attacked by Zachariah, Greg seemed broken. In that moment, Luke hadn't known what Greg was feeling, but now he did, and watching him here, standing tall, seeming so strong, Luke could only ask, "How did you get through it?"

"With you guys. I may be resilient, but I can't carry the weight of the world on my shoulders, and when I'm falling, you all help me up." Greg's gaze met Luke's own. "Will you let us do the same for you?"

He nodded. "Please, I-I can't do this on my own."

Greg walked over to him and squeezed his shoulder. "And you will never have to."

CHAPTER 4

Luke desperately wanted to rush into the warehouses in front of him, rip everyone apart, and find his mate. The hope in his chest promised him that Johanna would be here and the constant, endless, gnawing grief in his soul would ease, even if just a fraction.

But that was him speaking emotionally, and his emotions had done a number on his head.

He looked at Greg. One conversation wasn't going to change everything, but it did help. It had reminded Luke that he was better than this, and he would need to remember that in today's battle and the next. He needed to be logical here.

There was a big possibility that Johanna wouldn't be at this location, and from the poor state of the exteriors and broken windows which couldn't keep out the cold wind, he hoped she wouldn't be inside. The warehouses looked abandoned. Those with wood seemed rotted, warped, and filled with the elements of the nearby sea. The surrounding buildings seemed just as bad, their once silver metal now turned to rust.

But Luke and the rest of the battle officers believed these appearances to be a façade. This location had nine buildings from what they'd seen, and each was equipped with high quality cameras. While they hadn't heard anything or seen any vehicles or movement from outside the warehouse buildings, none of the buildings they'd scoped had dust in front of the door, which meant someone, somewhere, was indeed home.

Greg nodded to them, and Luke knew the game was on. He squeezed his hands, rotating his arms and rolling his shoulders back. Daniella moved beside him and caught his gaze. If anyone had told Luke a couple of months ago that his best friend would be on the front lines with them, he wouldn't have believed it. But Daniella's life had changed greatly in a short amount of time, and she'd been forced to change with it or become buried by it. Daniella had taken the existence of vampires and immortals, her new relationship, and dedication to their circle the same way she did everything else, with committed determination.

Dani gave him a soft, reassuring smile, but as she turned to the building closest to them, her smile changed into a vengeful grimace that sent a chill down Luke's spine. She wasn't bloodthirsty. She didn't enjoy killing others or being involved in this war—Luke knew that like he knew his own hand—but Daniella was an advocate for justice. Her wrath was prevalent in her abilities as she pulled the cold air toward her, creating a whipping gust that cut and sucked the warmth out of his body. That gust built into a mini tornado before it flew forward in the direction of each building. As it hit, the windows concaved to her power, sending shards of glass everywhere and slamming the doors open.

A click sounded from Luke's right, and he watched as the door exploded, flying off the building while a fire raged inside. They were far enough away that the blast wouldn't harm them, but the shockwaves and sound were jarring. Suddenly, the fire stalled its normal expansion, then shriveled and died.

Dani's doing.

She used her powers to build the wind again, and then sent it flying once more to each building to trigger the opening of any secret doors.

The second blast roused their adversaries, and at least twenty men appeared. Luke called his power to him. A fog rolled in from the sea, blanketing the area in shrouded mist. But there was a sound, metal singing through the air, and Greg surged forward, catching the knife that was meant for Daniella's head. At Greg's roar, they charged forward. Snarls and screams ripped through the air around him as Luke weaved through the enemy. The fog hid the bodies of those that fell, but he knew where each of his team members were.

As Luke cut the head off another vampire, ten more appeared. He vanished, dissipating into shadow. Luke slithered along the ground, jumping from place to place until he found Greg's shadow. His darkness curled around Greg, curving into his power, a signal they'd long forged between them to alert to disturbances. Greg gave a small nod. As soon as he reached out with his own energetic ability to alert the others, Luke was off, jumping and sprinting from one shadow to the next until he was behind the vampires. His blood sang with the need to kill them, but he had other duties to follow.

Luke found their exit, a cellar beneath one of the buildings that seemed to connect to the others. That meant that the other buildings were either decoys, traps, or escape routes. Luke kept to his shadowed form as he slipped inside, the fighting continuing in the open air. He raced along the walls, only pausing to inspect doorways for more traps.

Deeper down the tunnels he found two vampires. He killed one of them within seconds, but the other one's death he purposefully prolonged, cutting his arm off when he could have severed his head. The vampire screamed, giving Luke what he wanted. The sound would alert others that may be waiting.

When no one came, Luke cut off his other arm. The vampire fell to the ground, his cries of pain echoing so loudly they hurt Luke's own ears. Still, no one appeared. Satisfied, Luke gave the man mercy by cutting off his head.

Even though Luke had proved that the nearby area was clear, or that any lingering vampires were otherwise preoccupied, he knew he couldn't let down his guard. Zachariah loved to set traps. He got a sick satisfaction by trying to prove he was smarter than everyone else, and Luke was not about to give it to him. Doing the next best thing he could think of, Luke took the dead vampire's arms and carried them on his shoulder as he sunk back into his shadowed form. When he neared the next entrance, he threw one of the arms toward the top, spiraling it so that it would clear the doorway vertically, like a body. When no explosion or threat appeared, Luke reclaimed the arm from the floor and continued along.

Nearing another passageway, Luke threw the arm again and was surprised when someone caught it.

Merida stepped through the door frame and cringed at the limb in her hand. "Really?"

"Don't judge," Luke said as he rematerialized from his shadows. "It's a good way to test for traps. Your head didn't get blown off now, did it?"

Merida handed the appendage back to Luke and dusted her hands off, although he didn't know why—they were already covered in blood. "Yes, but you killed him. It's a little weird to use his limbs this way. It's kind of like violating the body."

Luke side-eyed her. "You're just mad that's the appendage I cut off. If it would have been his dick, you would have been happy."

Merida covered her mouth with the back of her hand, smothering her laughter. "You know what? You're right. But please don't ever do that. I can take a lot of things seriously, but dicks flying through doorways is not one of them."

Luke laughed deep from his gut. His eyes watered and he wiped them with the shirt's sleeves. "Duly noted."

Recovering, he straightened his back and took in Merida's appearance and the lack of Dom or any of his animal forms hanging off her. She noticed and nodded to the right. "Dom's checking out that passage. We've got four more minutes before Greg wants us topside."

Luke resumed navigating the passage with Merida in tow, and then she called out to him. He paused and turned toward her. "What is it?"

"There's something at the top of the opening. Probably an explosive."

Luke nodded. Taking a step back, he threw one of the deceased vampire's arms at the opening. The moment it passed through, the mechanism ticked and then exploded, causing the passage to shake as the vibrations bounced and pulsed through the air. Compacted dirt and boulders rained down, effectively closing the earlier opening.

Behind them a whistle sounded through the air, making Luke tilt his head to the side. But when he glanced at Merida and saw her small smile, he knew what, or rather who, had made the noise.

The sound of a bird's wings grew closer to them, and then feather turned to skin and bone as Dom's figure appeared in front of Merida. He wrapped his arm around her shoulders, pulling her close to his side while her own arm found its way around his waist. Their heads tilted toward one another as they kissed.

Luke turned his head from the display of affection to give them some semblance of privacy and to keep his thoughts of envy at bay. But even though they spoke quietly, Luke heard Dom's concern for his mate and Merida's reassurance that she was fine loud and clear. Luke's eyes closed, fingers tightening into fists as he fought against his racing, aching heart. He took deep breaths, not wanting them to see that he had such a clear weakness. That he was so...

Stop it! You're not weak. You didn't fail. The only way you do that is if you never get her back, and that's exactly what will happen if you continue to think this way. Enough! Enough...

Luke swallowed hard and plastered a neutral expression on his face as he addressed Dom. "How was your passage?"

"Riddled with explosives. It seems they split half of the passages into safe routes and the other half into traps. While I was in animal form, I heard Greg and Daniella closest to the passage you went down, Meri. Seems like they're waiting for us." Dom gave Merida's shoulder a squeeze before letting her go.

Luke nodded. "Then let's go."

He tossed the last remnant of the vampire he killed onto the ground and followed the couple out, hoping that the investigation at the other warehouse buildings had provided more information than they'd found down there.

———

Greg and Daniella's house was buzzing with activity. The rest of the battle officers had arrived, anxious and excited to meet their new teams. Normally, whoever was called to a fight fought with the rest of the unit as one team. It was a good plan, one which allowed for more people to be available should an issue or surprise arise, but assigning and working with teams in this new way was the dawn of a new era. It was a signal of trust, trust that each member knew what they were doing and would work to support the others within their groups.

It was also a sign that Greg was letting go of his tight grip on the reins. While everyone rested their weight upon Greg's shoulders, each battle officer had proven themselves to be capable of fighting, surviving, and saving those they thought were worth the cause over the countless years. It was a celebratory moment for everyone there, especially Greg, and no matter the sadness in his heart, Luke could feel the joy too. He smiled as he watched their members from the bar, and for the first time in several lonely months he felt the comradery and familial bonds that had woven between each person. Those bonds spread as the hours passed by. Normally, Luke would have partaken in them, but he had other, bigger things on his mind.

He flipped through the paperwork they'd retrieved from the warehouse raid. Most of it was from the building that had exploded prior to the fight. Thanks to Daniella's powers, several of the documents had been saved. Luke didn't know what he would find in them, so he did his best to curve any hope that it would lead to Johanna. Hope had begun to feel just as much of a vice as fear and doubt, so instead he let himself get lost in the details, information, coordinates, and connections. He recorded, filed, and sorted the paperwork into what made sense to him. His creative mind painted a picture, one that continued to grow and expand into something he was sure would lead to an answer.

"There's a lot of things I thought I would find you doing, but paperwork wasn't one of them," Dani said as she entered the room with a drink in her hand. She offered it to him, and he took it with a nod of thanks.

"Hey, just trying to make myself useful." Luke smiled, but at the look on her face it turned to a grimace.

Her eyes narrowed. "Say that one more time and see what's going to happen to you. You might be a vampire, but I can and will be more than happy to kick your ass."

Luke couldn't help but smile, even as she huffed. "You're right, I'm sorry." He sighed, leaning back in the chair. "On the plus side, Greg already chewed me out for being negative. Will that make you take pity on me?"

Dani pulled up a chair, turning the back of it to face him before she sat down, crossing her arms on the top.

"Technically speaking, I have been taking pity on you, even though you've been ignoring me."

"I have not—" He stopped at her glare and squeezed the bridge of his nose before softening more into the chair. "I'm sorry."

Dani looked him over before sighing as well. "It's okay. I understand, I do, and I know this isn't something I can fix for you. I also know Mya was worse. With Erik, I mean."

Luke gulped at the reminder of his cousin broken by the death of her mate. He had to clear his throat before he could speak. "I guess she was, but it's hard to see a difference between her and I right now." His gaze moved to the ceiling, studying the mosaic of lines and curves within the woodwork to try to silence his self-deprecating thoughts.

"There are differences," she said, and he met her eyes. "You still have hope, and you haven't given up. You're angry. You have every right to be, and I know how easy it is to turn that anger onto yourself, but you still have hope. You might think that's a weakness, but that's the hardest part of it all. That hope is your strength, Luke."

Luke stared at her, really stared at her for a moment. Then he stopped and thought about her circumstances. Daniella lost her mother when she was young, which had caused her to go into the foster system. That trauma was why she'd worked her ass off and hadn't made time for the small things that made her happy. While a parental bond was not a mate bond, the grief felt was the same, and even though Daniella was hundreds of years younger than himself and his family, at times she seemed to be wiser than all of them put together.

Dani squeezed his wrist with her hand. "I know you'll find Johanna and that the two of you will be a wonderful, beautiful couple. I don't need anyone to tell me that. I know because I believe in you. You helped me turn my life around, Luke, and I wouldn't have found the joy and love I have now without you."

Her eyes began to water, and Luke bit his lip to stop from succumbing to tears as well.

"You will get her back, Luke. I swear it. I'll help you get your mate, and once you have her, I'll help you keep her. I promise. Even if I have to scream your praises from the top of every rooftop to convince her. You're not alone. If you can't believe in yourself, believe in me. I won't let you down."

Luke wrapped his arms around her, and they sunk into the embrace as he tilted his head back to keep his tears at bay. Finally, when he could speak, he whispered to her, "I believe in you. Even if I can't believe in myself, I'll always believe in you."

CHAPTER 5

It hurt. Everything hurt. Every single piece of her felt as though it was both on fire and numb at the same time. Her legs barely moved on their own.

That she had made it this far was purely due to her will power. Johanna couldn't open her eyes to navigate. The only thing guiding her was the touch of the rough cavern wall. She'd lost the strength to stand away from it, and now allowed it to cut into her skin as she dragged herself forward, inch by inch. The protection of her clothing was gone, either from when Zachariah had torn it from her, her fight to break free, or taken by the wall itself. Each jagged curve of rock pressed into her skin, and the more she fought against the blackness calling to her, the more she allowed the wall to cut into her. The pain kept her awake, kept her alive, for now. But for how long was the question.

Zachariah knew. Somehow, he had found out that

she had leaked information. Johanna didn't think he was one hundred percent certain, but he suspected her, and that was enough to damage her body beyond repair. After all, how many times had he done it before?

A rock pressed against her wrist, causing her to hiss. She bit her lip, forgetting it too was busted, and winced as pain shot through her again. Still, she continued to move, but how much longer could she go on?

Why was she moving again?

Why wasn't she giving up?

She paused for a moment as a face came into her mind. Ah, him. That's why. Luke. *Her* Luke.

Some deity probably laughed at her claim over her mate. A man who deserved and could do much better than her. He wouldn't have wanted her even back when she was whole, back when her skin was not covered in cuts and stab wounds, serrated and hanging away from her body, back when she had not been tainted by Luke's very own enemy, when her mind, her very body, had not been stolen from her.

But still, Luke was hers, and in her dreams he wanted her. He was who she pictured when Zachariah abused her. It was Luke's arms she'd grown accustomed to as her safe place. It was him she envisioned when she entered the sanctuary of her mind, the one place that Zachariah couldn't reach, the place that her consciousness escaped to when he poisoned her. In Johanna's mind she could run her fingers through Luke's soft ash brown hair and she could stare into his green-gray eyes, the same eyes that made the whole world melt away until there was nothing left. If Luke saw her now, her once golden hair matted in blood, dirt, mud, and shit, her skin covered in the same suet, those eyes would harden. He'd be disgusted, as disgusted as she was with herself. Still, even though it would hurt, she wanted to gaze into those eyes one more time.

Johanna had done everything she could to help him, to protect him. She had even masked their mating bond until she'd seen him in the cave, until she had to feel him, had to connect with him just for a moment, even if it was the first and last time. She'd given up on being saved from Zachariah and had thought she'd accepted her fate to die at his hands. But even though that may be her destiny, she refused to let anyone else follow the same path. She'd saved people when she could, helped them escape, and controlled Zachariah's own vampire allies to allow their departure, so when he condemned someone, it would be them.

Perhaps that's why she never blamed the gods. Johanna was just like the villains who held her captive. She judged them and decided their lives were worth nothing. They were just as responsible for every injury, every scream she and the others endured. If those bastards died, Johanna's heart hurt for the lives they could have had, but the warrior in her soul—the one she had grown to be, the one who promised to outsmart her enemy at every turn— said "Good riddance." That's how far she'd fallen.

She had to stop herself from laughing at the irony of her circumstances. Johanna had been willing to die until the moment Zachariah tried to kill her. Then she wanted to live. Now, at this very moment, she wanted to breathe, to be free. But that wouldn't come for her. No. She was just as evil as they were, taking another's life and finding joy in their deaths.

She had become the very monster she strove to protect against.

Johanna sunk to her knees, her legs no longer working. Blood seeped out of her scrapes and cuts, but poured from the stab wound to her side, the one that she knew would kill her.

She rested her head back against the wall and cried silently, until finally she couldn't hear, couldn't feel, couldn't taste. She simply was. And in that moment, just one more time, she saw his face.

Goodbye, Luke. I'm sorry I never got to truly know you. I'm sorry I couldn't be the mate you deserved. But I hope, at least, with my death, you'll be free.

And then she slipped away into nothing but the cold, dark black.

———

Something felt off to Luke. It was a strange feeling under his skin, digging into his heart, which kept causing him to pause. It was as if something was calling to him, tugging him somewhere.

It gnawed at him as he left with his team for their battle. At first, he thought it might be a warning that something bad would happen during their raid, or that someone would get hurt or worse, and he warned his team because of it. But everything went off without a hitch. Every member played their part. They defeated the few vampires there and gathered all the intel they could, but still the feeling continued.

Luke and his team returned to Greg and Daniella's home, as expected. He set the files and a USB they had collected from the raid down on a table, alongside an SD card of pictures they had taken. His intent was to review them while they waited for the others, but then a lightning-like surge flew through his body, constricting around his muscles before fleeing, only to be replaced by the gnawing feeling clawing at him. It tugged him along until he mindlessly walked out the door and got in his car. Only then did he regain control.

Luke knew he should wait for the others, but this, whatever it was, felt as if he were running out of time. He had to go. He didn't know why, but he had to. Shifting his car into gear, he pulled down the driveway and then he was off, but that didn't make the feeling any better. Instead the feeling grew, spreading out from his heart through his torso until he clenched the steering wheel hard.

Something's wrong. What is this?

Luke did the only thing he could. He called Greg.

"Hey," Greg said, and Luke could hear him shuffling around. "We just got back. Where are you?"

"Something—" Luke coughed, trying to clear his throat as it suddenly felt hoarse and tight.

"Luke? What's wrong?"

"I don't know," he choked out, swerving around the bend of another curve as he followed the tug. "Something's leading me somewhere."

Luke coughed again, his eyes watering against the tightness in his chest. He heard Greg shout, starting a conversation in the background that Luke couldn't focus on.

"Mya just checked your GPS. You're heading home." Greg said.

"Home?"

"Yes." Another conversation carried on in the background before Greg spoke to him. "Can you try to take a deep breath, then try to describe the feeling."

Luke inhaled and exhaled, but it hurt. It was as if someone was breaking through his ribcage, trying to tear out his heart. "It feels like someone's ripping me apart." He cursed as another whip of pain went through him, another lash that squeezed. "Like a fucking snake is wrapped around my body and it's crushing me. It started in my heart and—"

He groaned, biting back a scream.

There was a murmur in the background, and then Greg shouted before coming back to him. "Luke, it's Johanna…"

"What?" Luke took a curve too fast, almost hitting the guard rail.

"We're coming." Another pause. "Try to push reassurance through the line. Push as hard as you can, okay? But we're coming."

At Johanna's name, panic mixed in with the feeling. "I don't understand—"

Greg's voice was steady and calm, but his words froze every cell in Luke's body, "Luke, she's dying. What you're feeling is the death of your mate."

Luke's eyes widened. His hands shook but he righted himself as he raced down the road faster than before, his body reacting quicker than his mind could process.

"Get home," Greg bit out. "We're coming. We're right behind you, but she needs to know you're going to be there, so push into whatever connection you feel with her, so she knows not to give up."

The roar of an engine ended the call, and the silence was louder than Luke's disbelief. It did feel like he was dying, like pieces of him were being hammered away, like he was fighting fate itself. But he would fight fate, the universe, the gods themselves if it meant he could save his mate, so he did. With every breath, he pushed against the tightness. Luke remembered the last time he had seen Johanna, how she had spoken to him telepathically, and he tried that. He'd try anything to get her to keep going.

"Johanna? Can you hear me?"

Nothing.

He tried again. *"Johanna?"*

Luke was met with silence, and he restrained himself from punching the steering wheel. He took another turn too quickly, his whole car shifting to one side as it lifted around a curve and then slammed back down, but he didn't care.

"I'm coming, baby. I'm coming. Please, whatever you're feeling, hold on for me, please."

Five minutes later, he pulled into the circular driveway of his home, and then he was out, dashing over the gravel and grass. He ran, using every ounce of his speed until he reached the back of his property where the pull was the strongest.

Luke's panicked state had him looking around for a standing human being, and then lower, scanning. The still air suddenly moved, and beneath the smell of flowers from his garden he finally scented her blood, and then he saw her.

Luke rushed to her, a gasp leaving his lips at the sight of his mate. In all his years, he had never seen someone so sullied and broken. He cradled Johanna in his arms, scanning her skin and taking in her injuries. Strands of her long, blonde, wavy hair were stuck to her face, covered in blood and other matter he could smell and feel beneath his fingertips. Her lips and nails were blue. There were finger marks, bite wounds, gashes and rope burns around her neck. Her clothes were tattered and shredded, and beneath them her skin hung drastically from starvation, caked in the same substances as her face and hair, making it difficult for him to take in all her wounds. Each breath she took was too shallow, too fast. Looking down, Luke watched as blood poured from the stab wound in her side.

He didn't want to move her in case her spinal cord or organs had been punctured, but he had to get her inside and laid down for Mya to assess and heal her body properly. As gently as he could, Luke picked Johanna up, cradling her head to his chest. He lifted his foot to kick in the door, not wanting to spare any time, but then he paused. Only the inner circle knew where he lived, and each of those members had met earlier to raid Zachariah's locations. How exactly had Johanna found her way to his home?

Luke turned back to scan the distance, but he didn't see anything. He took a long, deep breath, trying to see if he could smell another being, but it was only them. The only other living scent was a family of deer beyond the tree line, and they were no more interested in him than Luke was in them.

Despite that, he did have to agree that this would be the perfect trap. Johanna's state and the pain he fought against through their bond, even now, had blinded him from checking his surroundings or even his home. He decided that it didn't matter. Even if this were a trap, he had to save Johanna. Greg, Daniella, and Mya would be here soon, and even if he lost his life in the process, he refused to lose hers. He would need to be cautious though, to force his mind into overdrive even though his body and heart were breaking apart.

Luke shifted Johanna slightly to pull his keys out from his pocket and put them in the heavy, wooden back door. He turned the knob and twisted his body so he would get hurt in place of Johanna if someone were waiting for them or had planted a trap. When he slowly opened the door, nothing happened, and when Luke took another whiff of his space, searching for any being's scents that did not belong, he couldn't find any.

Satisfied, he moved to the nearest flat surface—his dining room table—and shoved everything off so he could lay Johanna down as gently as possible. She didn't groan, didn't make a sound as he adjusted her, and that scared him even more. He fixed her legs onto the table, being mindful of their gashes and split open flesh, then he looked her over. Her state of nakedness dawned on him, but he pushed the thoughts away as his eyes landed on her wound. He knew he would need to get clean blankets and a towel to hold against her side. He didn't want to leave his mate defenseless when she needed him the most, but he knew he had to while he still could. The pain in his body was growing, causing his muscles to clench and spasm, and he was worried that it may incapacitate him entirely.

Luke shrunk to his shadowed form, finding the fluidity easier to move in. He raced, slithering under baseboards and across rooms to grab blankets and towels before rematerializing beside Johanna. He pressed a towel to the wound at her side. With his other hand, he covered her. Even in this state, even with pain and fogginess marring his brain, Johanna was still beautiful to him, and he wanted to be the only one to see her body.

His fingers shook as he picked up his cellphone and called Greg. He waited for him to answer before saying, "Kitchen."

Greg grunted in response, his focus clearly on the road. "We'll be there in three minutes."

"Hurry, please." Luke swallowed, his voice sounding weak even to his own ears. "She's bleeding out."

Tires screeched in the background. "We're coming, hold on for me."

"Stay on the phone, Luke. We need to make sure you stay with us too," Dani said.

"Okay," Luke responded, but he wasn't really speaking to them. He couldn't seem to focus. Instead, he leaned down, his forehead touching Johanna's as he rubbed her cheek softly. Luke closed his eyes, breathing her in, not the blood, the sweat, the shit, or the other scents, but the essence of her that was hidden underneath it all.

"Johanna?" he called to her through their bond. *"You spoke to me like this once, and I'd give anything to hear your voice again."*

Luke paused in his stroking of her skin, grimacing as another lash of pain went through him. *"Was that you? Are you mad at me for not rescuing you, sunflower? Although it seems you didn't need me in the end."*

Another slice of pain, this one harder, sharper. *"Would you forgive me if I told you I'd give my life for yours? That I'd switch places with you if I could?"*

A lightning bolt of pain followed, so strong it left him gasping. His hand clenched the table as he breathed through the feeling, a broken smile forming at his lips. *"So it is you. Remind me not to make you mad in the future."*

The pain was still present and debilitating, but less intense.

"I know we didn't have the greatest beginning, Johanna. There are so many things I wish I could go back and do differently, but I don't believe this is our end. Please, give me a chance to show you what we could have together. Don't give up on me before we've even started."

The door to his house slammed open followed by a stampede of footsteps. *"The calvary is here, sunflower. I know this all must hurt so, so much, but please, just a little longer. I've been searching for you for such a long time. I can't lose you, not yet. Stay with me, please."*

Luke pulled back from her just as Greg, Daniella, and Mya came into the room. They paused for a split second, Daniella gasping while Greg and Mya cursed at Johanna's state, and then they flew into action. Mya and Daniella took turns at the table while Greg searched Luke's cabinets. Luke moved to help Greg, but he stopped him.

"Stay there, she needs you." Greg pulled out a bowl and cup, then began to fill one of them with water.

Luke nodded. "Okay. Mya, she has a stab wound on her right side." He lifted the blanket to show his cousin, who cursed again.

Daniella fished around in the drawer before handing Mya a sharp knife. Mya nodded in thanks and then slit a deep gash into her palm. She clenched her fist once, twice, before sliding her hand into the wound to speed its recovery.

"Would you do my other hand for me, please?" Mya asked Daniella.

Dani hummed in response, cutting into Mya's other hand. Greg brought the cup to her and laid in on the table. Mya put her hand on top of it, letting the blood drip into it while Greg and Daniella went around washing whatever cuts they could without raising the blanket further than was necessary. Once enough blood was in the cup, Mya handed it to Greg.

"Put it on whatever wounds you find so we can heal as many areas as possible at the same time," Greg instructed Daniella, and they set off working together.

Luke continued to run his fingers over Johanna's cheek, taking in her appearance and looking for changes. Her lips were still blue, her skin still pale and clammy. "Is she accepting your blood?"

"Yes, but it's going to take a while. We were really close to losing her, but I think she stayed around for you." Mya flexed her fingers again, sending more blood into Johanna. "You did well, Luke, but you're going to need some of my blood too."

He frowned at that. "I do? Why?"

"Because you look like you were on death's door with her. Your skin is pale, your eyes are glazed over, and I can hear your heart beating a mile a minute." Mya lifted her free hand to his mouth. "Drink."

Luke looked at her for a moment to judge if she was sure. When she narrowed her eyes, he clasped onto her arm and bit into her wrist. Blood squirted into his mouth, and he slurped it down. He squeezed her wrist as her healing magic hit him like a sucker punch, flowing through his veins and into the pathways that fed his organs. Every part of him felt revitalized, his vision clearer, hearing sharper, senses stronger.

Slowly Luke released Mya's wrist and found that the pain he felt before had vanished. Luke turned his gaze back to his mate. Johanna's skin seemed rosier, and his soul sung in praise. "Thank you."

"Where did you find her?" Greg asked as he continued to coat Johanna's wounds in Mya's blood.

"At my back door." Luke stroked his fingers over Johanna's hair. "I don't understand how she got here. I didn't sense anyone."

The mood in the room shifted as each of his family members went on high alert. Greg turned to Daniella. "Baby, could you check the environment while I make sure the house is clear?"

She nodded. "Of course."

Luke took the cup of blood from Dani's hands, and she closed her eyes, calling on her magic. Static electricity sizzled the air, making Luke's hairs stand on end as he tended to his mate. He kept his mind on Johanna, trusting Dani and Greg to be the supportive shield he needed right now.

"The house is clear," Greg said.

A few moments later, Dani said, "There's no one outside or in the surrounding land either."

"I don't know how she got here"—Luke looked over Johanna again—"but I'm happy she's here."

Beside him, Mya nodded and retracted her hand from Johanna's wound, healing the gash on her hand in the blink of an eye. "That's all that matters. She's here, safe, and she's healing."

Luke released the breath he didn't realize he was holding. "How long will it take her to recover?"

"Give her a few hours." Mya handed the cup to Greg who took it to the sink and began to clean up the items they'd used.

"Can I move her? I don't want her to wake up to ... this." Luke swallowed, gesturing to the evidence of Johanna's injuries.

Mya shook her head. "No, I wouldn't just yet. But if you have a loose shirt or jacket, we could put that on her."

"I'll change her." Luke brushed his fingers over Johanna's head, a gentle, light caress. "Dani, can you—"

"I've got it," she said, walking off in the direction of his bedroom.

Mya continued to gather the towels around Johanna before setting off to the laundry room. Luke called out to her, stopping her in her tracks. "Thank you for saving her."

Mya gave a stiff nod before she left.

Thank you for saving me.

CHAPTER 6

Five hours had passed. Johanna's breathing was mostly normal, which settled some of the fear in Luke's chest, but she was still unconscious. Sometimes her pulse raced under his fingertips, but it didn't seem to be from any type of external stimulus. She didn't respond to his voice, to him trying to initiate a telepathic connection with her, his touch, nothing.

Mya gave him the okay to get her cleaned up, knowing Johanna had enough of her blood in her system that any major damage would have been repaired. But even Mya was at a loss as to why Johanna wouldn't stir.

It's fine. Everything will be okay. Everything is okay.

His mate was under his roof, at his side, in his very arms. It was simply not possible that anything could be wrong, but if something was then he would fix it. For now, Luke would start with what he could control.

He carried Johanna into his bedroom, and didn't stop until he reached bathroom and shut the door behind them. Luke rested her in a corner and drew them a bath before removing the blanket he'd wrapped her in. Then he began gently peeling away the stuck remnants of her clothing. He kept glancing at her face, just in case she opened her eyes in the middle of him undressing her, but she did not.

Luke removed his own clothes, gathered the garments together and tossed them into the trash. Even if they could be salvaged and the blood removed, he did not want the reminder of how he'd found his mate.

With the tub quickly filling, he added soap and brought an array of devices over to the side of the tub for his task before lifting his mate and easing them both into the hot water. Johanna's relaxed body melted against his and he had to blow out a harsh breath at her nearness. Months of emotions bubbled to the surface and for just one moment, he hugged her to him. Tears slid down his face as he buried his head in her neck to breathe her in.

For so long he'd looked for her, searched for her, thought about her, dreamt about the last time he'd seen her, fantasized about her and about what life could possibly be like with her at his side. Even his body, traitor that it was, reacted to her. Even though they were both filthy, he still wanted her *desperately*. Having her in his arms stirred the need to bite her, to take her and make her his, but that wasn't right, not like this. He would not touch her, ever, until she was awake, had consented to their bond, and wanted him in the same way he wanted her. Until then, no matter how long it took or how long he had to wait for her to awaken, he would stay by her side, watch over her, protect her, spoil her, treasure her, and cherish her. He knew it like he knew his own name. And if he was lucky, during that time he'd get to know her and the bond between them would go from being something that marked her as his mate to her being the woman he loved fiercely.

Luke swallowed his emotions back, devoting himself to the task at hand. He picked up the scrub brush and went to work, dipping it into the hot water before pouring soap onto it and scrubbing Johanna's back. The strands of her hair were stuck there at first, but the hot water loosened them enough to allow him to slide them over her shoulder. He scrubbed her, cleaning away the filth that marred her flesh until her light skin was rosy pink.

Luke moved thoroughly from place to place, sometimes having to go over one section of her back multiple times before getting it clean. Finally, when he could no longer see beneath the water to clean the top of her ass, he shifted her and drained the tub before filling it and starting the process over again.

Five washes later, he had cleaned the majority of her body while doing his best not to focus on her creamy skin and luscious curves. Mya's blood had not only healed her wounds but filled the spaces of her body that had concaved from starvation. She wasn't back to the weight he'd seen her at before, one that made her hips full, thighs thick, ass abundant, and stomach curved in a way that made him want to gather it into his hands and squeeze its softness, but at least she was on her way.

Luke stood with her, carrying her to the shower to wash her hair. The waist length tresses were at least a little cleaner from the bath, but her scalp needed a good scrub to lift away the last of the debris. Gently he scrubbed her scalp with shampoo several times, then conditioned and detangled her hair while still in the shower. Only after he was done with her did he finally wash himself as well, a reprieve that had his hardened cock settling down a little.

After drying off his mate and himself, he dressed Johanna in one of his shirts and a pair of his boxers, making a mental note to get her comfortable clothes to wear around the house. Then he dressed himself before making the tough decision to lay her down in a spare room instead of his own bed. One day she would willingly lie there, but until then he wanted her to be comfortable and feel safe with him.

Johanna still hadn't awoken, and if she didn't soon they'd need to get more medical supplies to give her liquid nutrients. Luke setup the IV for vitamins and nutrients and added a nasogastric tube for Johanna, just in case.

Settling the sheets and comforter around her, he sighed heavily. "I don't know what you're going through," he said softly, "but I'm here. You're safe here and I promise to take care of you."

Luke kissed her head before stepping out of the room to find his family. As he approached Mya, Dani, and Greg, he took in the tenseness of their shoulders and realized something else had occurred.

"What happened?" Luke asked.

Dani's hand slid away as Mya's posture grew straighter, her lips thinning. "Nothing," Mya said. "How's Johanna? Is she awake yet?"

"No." Luke took a seat at the table, his eyes touching Greg's own. Luke could sense sympathy and anger in them, but it didn't feel as though either emotion was just for him. "What's going on?" Luke asked again.

"Nothing," Mya bit out.

"Mya—" Dani started.

Luke cut her off, his hand clenching into a fist. "I'm not going to sit here and act like I believe whatever lie you're trying to tell yourself." He paused, thinking back to earlier when he'd thanked her. Mya always had a difficult time accepting thanks, and he thought the fact that his mate had been saved while hers hadn't might have been the cause for her gruff behavior, but now he knew better.

"Luke," Greg said carefully, "why don't we go into another room to talk?"

Mya's head snapped up as she bared her teeth. "Just say it here! Let him know! Don't try and fucking coddle me!"

"Then don't give me a reason to!" Greg shouted, causing Mya to jerk back into her seat at his explosion.

Dani's hand squeezed Mya's shoulder, and that was all it took for Mya to break down, tears streaming over her bronze skin.

"Let's go, okay?" Dani said softly.

She nodded and Dani helped her out of her chair, leaving Greg and Luke to listen to Mya's sobs and Dani's placating words echoing down the hall. It had been a long time since Luke had seen Mya so distraught, so broken.

"Greg, what the fuck happened?"

Greg clasped his hands together, then brought them up to his lips. He took a deep breath before locking his eyes on Luke. "When you told us what you were feeling earlier, Darius was the one who recognized it as the loss of your mate."

Luke shook his head. "Okay?"

"We thought a mate could only physically feel that loss if they had consummated their relationship and satisfied the mate bond, something you never got the chance to do."

"Where are you going with this?" Luke asked.

"Mya has never felt what you did, Luke. Ever. If Erik

was her mate, which we know he was, and he died, she should have felt that even without their bond being consummated."

Greg sat back in his chair with a sigh, squeezing the bridge of his nose before fixing his eyes back on Luke.

"For three hundred years she's been mourning a death that never happened. He's alive, Luke. Erik is alive."

CHAPTER 7

He was running out of options. A week had passed and Johanna was still unconscious. Luke stayed by her side nearly every minute of the day, not wanting to miss the moment she opened her pretty blue eyes, but it never happened. Johanna was still responding to some sort of mental stimulus, twitching her face every so often, scrunching her cute pert nose, wrinkling her forehead, and even breaking out into a cold sweat, but she just wouldn't open her eyes. It wasn't truly a coma as her body seemed to be functioning, but it was as if she was under some sort of spell.

While Luke had watched over her and taken care of her, he browsed the books and articles he had on magic, lore, witches, and witchcraft. When they gave him no answers, he reached out to anyone he could think of from their inner circle with an ability that might be able to help.

Greg had the ability to look into past memories, but both he and Luke knew they could not use his power on Johanna. When Greg used that ability without permission, it ripped the person apart, locking them into a type of mental paralysis while he forced the scenes to play for the both of them. As Johanna was not fully catatonic and she at least had the ability for telepathy, there was a small chance she may be able to give Greg mental permission, but it wasn't a risk they were willing to take.

Dani was much the same. While she'd been learning how to use her powers on a scientific level, she explained to Luke that working with someone's memory was complex. Still, when she came over to check on him and make sure he was taking care of himself, or fill in the gaps where he wasn't, she tried using her magic on him. Thus far she'd been able to look into some of his short-term memories, but Dani had no control over what she saw and had a hard time pulling herself out without affecting him as well.

Luke couldn't get a hold of Mya. She wasn't returning his calls or answering his texts or emails. According to Dani and Greg, she'd gone off the deep end in her search to find Erik, tearing through their archives, hacking agencies, and setting off on solo missions only to come back empty-handed and covered in blood.

Jason had seen Johanna. He'd cautioned Luke against getting his hopes up as his specialty was to hurt, not heal, but still Luke appreciated the effort. And for that effort, Jason had been flung back against a wall the moment he tried to look inside Johanna's head. When he'd recovered, Jason told Luke that there was a large mental barrier around her that he couldn't break through. Jason also guessed Johanna was cognizant enough to know Luke was beside her and not someone else, or else she would have lashed out at him too.

That news should have made Luke feel some sort of elation, but it only confused him more. What was she protecting herself from if she knew he was here with her? Was she trying to figure out if he would hurt her as well? If so, why would she leave her body open to him but not her mind? And there was still the lingering question of how she ended up on his property.

Astrid was finally able to see Johanna toward the end of the week. Luke was happy when Dani arrived at his house before her. He needed the support, and Astrid was his last hope. If she couldn't figure out what was going on, he wasn't sure what his next steps would be.

"Thank you for being here," Luke said as Dani pulled up a chair beside him.

She smiled. "Where else would I be?" Her gaze left his and moved to Johanna's form. "Has anything changed?"

Luke shook his head. "No. Her pulse is the same, heartbeat the same, breathing patterns all the same. Her hand fidgeted for the first time today though."

"Well, that's something." Dani's tone was light, hopeful, but Luke struggled to put stock in it.

The chime of his doorbell interrupted their conversation. Dani gave his hand a hard squeeze, then headed to the door to let Astrid in.

Luke stood, plastered a smile on his face, and gave her a tight hug once she entered the room. "Hi, Astrid."

"Hello, Luke," Astrid said. Then she recoiled, shuddering as if something disgusting had touched her.

Luke moved to ask her what was wrong, but then he realized her gaze wasn't on him, it was on Johanna's form.

"You don't have to be so feisty," Astrid huffed, coming to stand beside the bed.

Luke shared a look with Dani, but she shook her head and shrugged. "Astrid, who are you talking to?" he asked.

"Your mate. She's quite protective over you."

Luke's eyes widened. "What?"

Astrid didn't turn to him. Instead she looked at Dani, her head cocked to the side in question. "I'm surprised you don't feel it too."

Dani's gaze shifted between Astrid and Luke. "Feel what?"

Astrid made a soft humming sound before she slowly twiddled her fingers a few inches above Johanna's body as if she was plucking the strings of an instrument. Astrid paused around Johanna's waist, near the wound that had almost killed her. "Ah I see.

You were there when Luke brought her in. You helped save her."

"Yes, I did," Dani confirmed, her tone full of questions.

Instead of taking his earlier spot, Luke sat on the corner of the bed. He knew he was crowding Astrid, but for some reason he felt compelled to be as close to Johanna as possible. There was an electricity in the air, a call that made the hairs on his arms stand straight, and it called for him to protect his mate, even though he knew she was perfectly safe.

Astrid gave him a knowing smile but didn't say a word. When she reached the crown of Johanna's head, Astrid pulled back and considered her. She hummed again before taking Luke's seat, her face practically beaming. "Your mate, while unconscious, has very strong mental abilities, and she is protecting you and everyone you come in contact with."

"How?" Luke didn't even realize he had reached for Johanna's hand until it was clasped in his. The sudden feeling of her skin on his surprised him, but he couldn't fathom pulling away.

"Johanna is watching over this room, even this house. When I walked in, I felt as though I was being watched, and then I felt pressure when we hugged, as if someone was trying to push me back and away from you." Astrid made a circle with her hand. "All of that, was your sweet—although possessive and jealous— mate."

Luke studied Johanna. She seemed so still, even relaxed, except for her chest. Her breathing had changed, grown faster as if her adrenaline was rising.

"What does that all mean, Astrid?" Dani asked.

Astrid sighed, settling back in the chair. "It means that the magic that is keeping her unconscious is her own."

"How do I get her out of it?" Luke asked.

"You don't," Astrid replied, her voice sharp. "You cannot force her out of the magic. She has to feel safe enough to break it all on her own."

Luke turned in Astrid's direction, ready to speak, but she stopped him with the stillness in her normally swirling silver eyes. "Johanna has ... she's gone through a lot, Luke. And I think throughout that time, even though the two of you were not together, she relied on any memory or thought of you to ... separate herself from her trauma. She used you as her saving grace. But something tells me she also spent a lot of time protecting you, which is why she's like this now. She's stuck at a crossroads between those two thoughts. I don't think she realizes that she's not in hell anymore."

Luke clenched his jaw, grinding his teeth to keep from shouting his rage. He was so incredibly tired of it being this way for them. Johanna deserved more and Luke wanted to give it to her, but yet again she was somewhere he couldn't reach her.

He took a deep breath. "What can I do?"

"I think you're already doing a good job," Astrid said

carefully. "She just needs a little more time. Has she responded to you in any way?"

Luke shook his head. "She moves a little sometimes. Small things. Expressions, mostly. I thought they were signs she was coming out of it, but they don't seem to be, and they don't seem to be responses to me either."

"What about the day you found her?" Astrid asked.

Luke paused, thinking back. "Not really. I felt where she was." He twirled a piece of Johanna's hair around his finger. "And at some point I spoke to her, and the pain of losing her would either get stronger or weaker as if she was responding to me. But I haven't felt, heard, or seen anything that seems like a response since."

"Maybe ..." Dani began, meeting Astrid's eyes. At her nod she continued. "Maybe you're wrong, Luke. Maybe when she moves, she is responding to you in her own way, and when she can't, she sends the thoughts through you."

"What do you mean, Dani?" Luke asked.

"What you're doing right now, the way you're touching her. In all the time I've been here, you've never done that. You tend to sit beside her"—Dani nodded to the chair—"not this. Maybe, you're responding to her mental abilities. Since she can't touch you, she's asking you to touch her."

Astrid nodded. "That's exactly what I think is happening. Johanna clearly acknowledges you as her mate. She's protected you for a long time, and I think it's ingrained in her to continue to do so. Because Daniella,

Greg, and Mya were here when you found her and helped to save her, Johanna has decided they're safe. She can sense they provide you comfort as well, and because of that she trusts them. But other people will not feel welcomed the same way you all do, not until she deems them safe as well."

Astrid crossed her legs, resting her head on her palm. "What you're doing right now is responding to her pull. Your bond works like a conduit. The same magnetic system but on a mental and emotional level, most likely due to Johanna's powers. And I'm sure that when she does wake up it will be even stronger."

Luke bit his lip but nodded. It made sense, and if he were honest, he liked it. He liked knowing there was a secret connection between them, that Johanna knew and accepted him as her mate and trusted him to look out for her when she needed time to rest. He supposed, in a way, maybe that's all this was. That was the mindset change he needed, the swing toward the positive.

Johanna would need time to heal from everything that happened to her, just like she would need time to see that they could work together. This was the beginning of that, her time to rest and recover her strength. If she was cognizant enough to orchestrate all of this, then she was aware enough to awaken on her own. He just needed to give her time, and that was something he could do.

A smile graced his lips as he turned to Astrid. "Thank you. I feel like you've given me the answers I needed." Luke's gaze shifted to the floor with a sigh. "I've been drowning for a while with all of this, and sometimes it felt like I couldn't reach the surface no matter how hard I tried to swim."

"That's understandable," Dani said, and he met her dark brown eyes. "You have every reason to feel that way. Just try to remember that no matter how dark it gets in those moments, you're not alone. We're right there with you. We're reaching out to you, and we will always make sure you're safe. You can breathe, Luke. You can breathe."

CHAPTER 8

Luke's heart felt lighter as he said goodbye to Dani and Astrid and walked back into Johanna's room. For a moment he just stood there, observing her. He tried to see if he could feel the energy or presence Astrid had when she first arrived. He knew it was probably stupid to try, but he had to, because feeling Johanna in any way was better than not feeling her at all.

Luke approached the bed hesitantly. He had vowed to keep a respectable distance away from her until she was awake and able to consent to his touch, but even without feeling the pull from her again, he knew he needed this, *they* needed this. He sat on the bed instead of the chair. His hip pressed against her own as he captured her hand in his and leaned over her.

She was still, breathing normally, her golden hair spread around her shoulders and beautiful body like an angel. Angelic though she might be, Luke now knew that his little angel had fire in her. Luke breathed in her scent before brushing his fingertips through her mane, following the long tresses until they ended and curled around her waist. He traced back up the path until he reached her face, then caressed the softness of her full cheeks. He slid down her jaw, her throat, and stroked her pulse, feeling it thump against the pad of his thumb. He ended at her shoulder, and drew back just slightly, so he could take in more of her with his gaze.

"I wasn't sure if I wanted a mate," Luke began, then paused, shaking his head. "That's not true. I didn't want to find my mate. I was terrified to."

He rested his foot on the tufted frame of the bed and continued. "When I was a kid, I thought my whole world had ended. I'd lost my mother to the plague, my aunt and uncle had fallen ill, and Greg was forced to leave us and join the army. Even though I had no concept of death at the time, I fully expected to contract the plague and end up like my mother."

Luke stroked the back of Johanna's hand. "But then Greg came back as a vampire. He saved us, and I was grateful. I was grateful to him and Erik for letting me be a child, and I kept that mentality far into my twenties as a vampire."

He sighed. "I was restless, jumping from one thing to the next, gathering all the knowledge I could. I needed experiences to feel alive because I never imagined being able to live forever. I think," his voice quieted, "no, I know that for a while there, I thought I was invincible."

Luke took a deep breath, his shoulders sinking forward as he continued with his story. "I still thought I was invincible when the wars started. I bathed myself in the blood of others without batting an eye, because they were trying to take the one thing that mattered to me: my way of life. Greg, Mya, Erik, they were all part of that. Being a vampire has its perks, yes, but the biggest drawback is watching the faces of people you grow to care for die. I couldn't, I *wouldn't,* let anyone take another person from me, and I used every ounce of my false invincibility to do so. And then we started saving people."

Luke's eyes met Johanna's face, and even though her own eyes were closed, he still stared at them as if he could will them to open, as if he could connect to her, to make her understand him. "Do you know what it's like to save someone's life, to see them believe they're going to die and then give them another chance to live? That ... that did something to me."

"I started to change. I learned everything I could from doctors and surgeons who risked their lives on the front lines to heal their armies. I learned how to build shelters, houses, even hospitals, so that others could have somewhere to turn to. That's when I became terrified of having a mate, because I learned that I couldn't save everyone. Immortal didn't mean invincible, and it didn't mean I was an omniscient god. I couldn't always be there, and there was a possibility that one day my mate would need me and I couldn't be there to save her, to save *you*."

Luke ran a frustrated hand through his hair and sighed again. "I kept myself busy in every possible way I could. I do that a lot. When I'm stressed, I need to keep my hands busy, keep my mind elsewhere. It worked for a while, until Mya lost Erik."

He turned her hand in his, rubbing the space between her thumb and index finger, feeling a sense of comfort that logically he knew he must have imagined, but nonetheless wanted to believe was real.

"Erik was a father figure to all of us and losing him changed something in us. For me, it was the chaotic way I went after things, the way I obsessed when I didn't know what else to do. But it damn near killed Mya. For once, someone needed me and I didn't want to let her down. We were like that for a long time, until Dani, and now you. Mates are very rare for us immortals, and whether we meet our mates is entirely up to chance. We never know where, or why, or how."

Luke smiled. "But you, sweet little sunflower, walked into my life, infected my mind, and you haven't left it since, even when I didn't know you were my mate. So, while I find it incredibly adorable that you're chasing women out of my—and what I hope you'll accept to be your—house, you should know they never stood a chance." He brushed her cheek with his thumb.

"Because I am yours, Johanna, just as much as you are mine, and when you come back to me, I will spend my days reminding you of that in every way I can."

———

"Thank you for picking up the wallpaper," Luke said to Dani as he joined her at her green SUV.

Dani smiled, unlocking the trunk for him. "You're welcome."

While Luke began to grab the rolls and other supplies, Dani picked up several large bags from the backseat. Luke tilted his head to look inside them, but she swerved around him before he could ask.

Luke rolled his eyes and huffed as he followed her into his house, where she was already busy unloading the bags in Johanna's room.

"Are you going to tell me what else you got?" Luke asked as he set the wallpaper rolls down on the floor.

"A little bit of this, a little bit of that," Dani said in a sing-song voice as she bobbed her head, sending her dark brown curls swaying left to right. She blew him a kiss when he eyed her suspiciously. Then Luke saw her pull out a bundle of clothes.

"Are those for Johanna?" he asked.

"Yes. While I'm sure you get some weird, sick sort of alpha male satisfaction from having her in your clothes, she should have some of her own."

He was, in fact, satisfied every time he changed Johanna into his clothes, but that was beside the point. "How did you figure out her size?"

When Luke had casually mentioned to Dani that he wanted to hire a seamstress to measure Johanna so he could purchase clothing for her, Dani had nearly cut his head off. According to her, there were some things a woman had to volunteer on her own, and her clothing size was one of them. Luke thought it was ridiculous, especially since he was only asking to make his mate more comfortable, but Dani told him she'd take care of it.

"There's a reason why those high-end expensive stores have personal shoppers," she said as she put away another set of clothes, something pink catching his eye. As Dani headed back outside, she stopped and looked over her shoulder at Luke. "I like the new furniture by the way. It's very warm ... cozy."

To keep his mind off when Johanna might regain consciousness, Luke had kept himself busy. At first, he sketched Johanna, mixing her form with outfits and small details he remembered from when she would flit in and out of the office. It had been months since he'd felt that type of inspiration, and he was grateful that having her with him, even in this state, helped him find it again.

He'd also finished all his creative projects at work, setting the firm three weeks ahead. Then he pruned his garden and even designed a new plot on his property for future vegetables. He was regularly cooking again, sending Daniella and Greg home with dinners and desserts, or eating with them on the occasions they joined him in his home to catch up.

But now he had turned his attention to making this space into something he hoped Johanna would like. He didn't really know her tastes, so he focused all his choices around one picture. On her first day at The Novak Firm, IT had taken a picture of her for her badge. In it, her hair had been in a low ponytail, the curls slung over her shoulder. She wore a yellow cardigan and knee length black dress covered in daisies. Her lips had a subtle tint, making them seem pinker, and she may have worn some makeup around her eyes, but nothing else. In the picture, she was smiling. It was the only time in the four months she'd worked at The Novak Firm that Luke could remember her genuinely smiling. Something about that photo stuck with Luke, and he wondered if that was the last time she'd been free from all of this. If it was, then Luke would use that knowledge to help her feel not only safe here, but welcomed.

He had added beadboard halfway up the wall. While he'd waited for the wallpaper to come back in stock, Luke purchased furniture that he'd repurposed in a soft pale green color. He chose pale yellow and white curtains, which matched the other accent pieces—a chair, pillows, and comforter set—that he'd ordered.

According to his research, the aesthetic was called 'bohemian farmhouse,' but it just reminded him of his nickname for Johanna: sunflower.

Luke thumbed one of the bags Dani brought in before she walked back into the room with several more. "How much did you buy?"

She waved her hand dismissively at him, then pulled out a few bottles of shampoo and conditioner, followed by some new brushes.

Luke crossed his arms. "I already have those."

"No, what you have is shampoo and conditioner for straight hair, like yours. Johanna's hair is curlier and a closer texture to mine, so she needs different products."

Luke pouted, and Dani laughed. "You're doing a great job, Luke, I'm not saying you're not. I'm just going to teach you how to do a better one. Curly hair, even a texture not as tight as mine, needs a whole different routine. Think of it this way—if nothing else, you'll know how to do your children's hair if it's curly like Jo's."

Luke fumbled, dropping the bottle he was handing to Dani. She caught it, took one look at him, and burst out laughing. "You're blushing!"

"Shut up!" He threw a loofah at her when she laughed even more. "You're the one who brought up children. Where did that come from?"

"Oh, I don't know, probably the little birdie who told me how much of a horn dog you used to be. I knew you were a freak, but damn, Luke! What were you trying to test the theory of, use it or lose it?"

"I swear I fucking hate you." Luke rolled his eyes, but there was a grin on his face that grew until he finally laughed right alongside Dani. It felt good. He wasn't sure if it was the laugh, finishing this project for Johanna, or what, but there was a glee in the air, and for the first time Luke let himself feel it.

———

It had been a good night. Dani and Greg had stayed for dinner, beef Wellington with scalloped potatoes, carrots, and garlic butter biscuits. They'd talked for a while before Dani promised to come over tomorrow with Greg following later in the afternoon.

Luke pushed them out the door when they tried to help him clean up. He didn't want them to see what had become his nightly routine of saving a plate for Johanna, just in case today was the day she woke up. He always packed a sealed container and stored it in his refrigerator. If she didn't wake by the next morning, he would freeze whatever he could or eat the serving for lunch. To others it might be pathetic, but to Luke it was all a part of taking care of his mate. Hopeful delusions still involved hope, and he liked that a lot more than he liked being angry.

Nothing had changed when Luke entered Johanna's room, so he kissed her head and settled into the chair beside her bed for a little while, sketching her again. This time she was a spirit, a beautiful muse whispering in her lover's ear, inspiring his thoughts at all hours of the day, which wasn't far from the truth.

Eventually, his lines became sloppy as his eyes grew tired. With a sigh and one more look at Johanna, he picked up his sketching materials and deposited them in his studio. After taking a shower and changing his clothes, Luke grabbed his pillow and blanket from his bedroom and carried them through to Johanna's room, laying them out on the couch.

A small shuffle made him turn to look at the bed. Johanna's eyes were still closed, but he came over to her anyway. He stood by her side for a few moments before sitting down on the bed and taking her hand in his. Then he tucked a piece of her golden hair behind her ear and whispered, "You're safe. I'm right here, and I'm not going anywhere. You're not alone anymore, I promise."

Luke leaned down to kiss her forehead goodnight, but when he pulled back ocean blue eyes stared up at him. For a solid minute he didn't move, didn't speak, didn't breathe.

Please don't be a dream, please don't be a dream. That's too cruel. Please be real.

"Johanna?" He said her name softly, scared that if he spoke louder all of this would somehow be whisked away.

She blinked, opened her mouth, closed it, then opened it again.

"Luke?" she managed quietly.

His heart skipped a beat, his muscles tensed and every cell in his body came alive. He had to close his fist around her pillow to keep from yanking her into his arms. "You're awake!"

CHAPTER 9

"A-Awake?" Johanna asked.

Her throat was dry. Each time she swallowed, her saliva felt thick, sticky, but the feeling worsened when she looked into Luke's gray-green eyes. She couldn't look away from them. They captivated her. Every second that passed they broke through some unknown barrier, sinking deeper and deeper into her soul. He was leaning above her, supported by the arm beside her head. His stomach lightly rubbed against hers every time he took a breath, every time *she* took a shaky breath.

He was undeniable.

While having a mate wasn't something typical between a witch or psychic pair, Johanna knew all about mate bonds. She knew what they felt like, what they pushed for, and it was clear to her that not only were they mates, but their bond was incredibly strong.

It flowed through her, lighting her body aflame. Every piece of her felt as if it had been dormant for weeks, months, *decades,* but was now shocked awake.

His lips twitched, drawing her gaze as they spread into a slow smile. She had to bite her lip to keep from doing something stupid, like moaning. Then she parted her own lips and he inhaled, as if stealing the very air that left her. When she licked her lips, he bent forward, closer, and she wanted a taste just as badly as he seemed to. Beside her, the pillow tilted as Luke gripped it tight, but the hand near her hip that covered her own caressed her skin so softly, so featherlight yet achingly familiar.

Why did this feel familiar? When have we done this before?

The thought died in her mind as he neared her. Johanna lifted her hand, fingers aching to touch his face, to pull him closer and align with him, but the action made her hiss as something jabbed the inside of her arm. That single sound cut through the overwhelming chemistry between them, and Luke pulled away, leaving Johanna somewhere between gratefulness and disappointment. She moved to sit up, and Luke inched toward her. At the widening of her eyes, he grinned.

"Let me help you."

A shy smile spread across her lips before she nodded. Being mindful of what she now recognized were IVs in her arms, she placed her hands on Luke's broad shoulders, feeling his muscles tense under her touch. A blush spread across her skin, and she tilted her head away.

Luke wrapped his arm around her to support her as she slowly sat up. He fluffed her pillow before sliding to the side of her. Then his arms were under her body, and Johanna squeaked as he picked her up with ease. This was the first time in her adult life someone had moved her without a second thought, but Luke carefully placed her down against the headboard as if she weighed nothing. She wiggled, settling into the mattress. He still had a gleeful smile on his face, almost like he held a secret, something she'd forgotten. Whatever it was, she could tell it meant the world to him.

Johanna took a moment to look at him then, really look at him. His hair was wet, slightly wavy, while the ends held a curl. The dark strands fell to his eyes. He had high cheekbones, like a regal king, and she liked how the flesh around them changed when he smiled. She liked his lips too, liked how full and wide they were. His beard was a shadow around his face, connecting all the pieces together in a map Johanna wanted to follow with her fingers.

Her gaze traveled lower, taking in the span of his neck, his corded muscles big enough to show strength, but not overdone. They were muscles with a purpose. Johanna could tell Luke was a protector. He wouldn't hesitate to run into a burning building for someone he loved.

Suddenly, Johanna wanted to be that person. She wanted to be protected by him, wrapped in his strong arms, pressed against the width of his chest. She wanted to trail her fingers down his cut abs ... No, she wanted to taste them, to follow the panes of his body with her tongue until she reached—

"See something you like?"

Johanna jumped. Her eyes met Luke's and found them swimming with a mixture of amusement and something darker, more intense. She turned away, knowing she was blushing again, and heard his soft laugh. He took hold of her wrist, drawing her attention back to him, and motioned to the IV in her arm. "Let me take these out for you to help you feel a little more comfortable."

She nodded as he removed the tape.

"This will only hurt for a moment, okay?" Luke pulled the needle out and Johanna let out a soft hiss. But then he bent forward, and she watched in shock and fascination as he closed his mouth over the growing drop of blood. He swiped his tongue over it and her toes curled under the blanket. A second and third swipe had her clenching her thighs together, but then he pulled away.

Luke wouldn't look at her, and his movements were stiff as he began to remove the patches and equipment that had been monitoring her. Their disconnection triggered a loud beep, and with a sigh Luke got up to unplug the machine. Only then, with distance between them, did his eyes touch hers, so dark in the low light, and Johanna realized that he could smell her desire.

"Do you need anything?" Luke asked, his voice low, seductive.

The implication behind his words had Johanna fisting the comforter in her hands. Taking a deep breath was a mistake because she could smell him everywhere, including on her. As she swallowed, she was reminded of how dry her throat was and that it needed *actual* liquid. "Could I get a glass of water, please?"

"Of course. Would you like something to eat too?"

Johanna had to put a hand over her heart to stop it from pounding out of her chest. That question might have been simple to anyone else, but a man had never looked at her and asked if she wanted to eat. It was always that she should eat less, that she was 'so pretty' with her blonde hair, blue eyes, and pale skin, that if she just lost a little weight she could be anything she wanted to be, that she would be taken seriously if she put effort into the way she looked.

Even though Johanna promptly cut off anyone who said that to her, it didn't mean their words didn't hurt. The world had eaten her self-esteem and spit out the woman she was now, the one who couldn't fathom why anyone would look at her the way Luke had, not once, not twice, but three times in the ten minutes they'd been alone together. It could have been the mate bond —a rational explanation—but when she saw his concerned gaze, she knew that wasn't fully the case.

The mate bond only pushed the two people connected by it to consummate the bond. It didn't create feelings. It didn't force someone to care.

That realization softened her, and she smiled at Luke. He seemed awestruck by that, which made her laugh. Finally she said, "I'm not hungry yet, but thank you."

He seemed speechless for a moment, making her giggle again. Then he shuffled toward the door. "I'll be right back."

Johanna was still smiling when he left, until her eyes connected with the door frame and the decoration around it. The floral wallpaper was her style, and the same could be said for the furniture in its green hues. It reminded her of a garden, but while it was beautiful, it wasn't a room she was familiar with. She also hadn't heard any other voices or movement so far in the house. Johanna closed her eyes and tried to connect with anyone who may be on the premises, but the only person she found was Luke. This had to be his house, so why was she here?

Again it felt like she was missing something. She tried to remember, but it all seemed to be hidden from her, stuck behind some imaginary boulder that she couldn't move or pass through. She tried harder, closing her eyes again, her eyebrows furrowing as she focused inward, advancing, pressing on the mental block. When she did, she cried out, flying forward in the bed and into Luke's sudden arms.

"Johanna? What's wrong?"

She wailed, sobs tearing from her body and spilling into his. Johanna felt like she had been struck by lightning; her nerve endings were on fire, burning away until they shriveled and died.

Luke pulled her closer, rocking her in his arms while she burrowed her head into the crook of his neck. He stroked her hair as he gently shushed her. "It's okay, sunflower, you're safe. It's okay. I promise it's all going to be okay."

Sunflower?

The single world delivered a second shock to Johanna's system, causing her to freeze. He had been the one who saved her. His voice had led her out of her own personal hell. Every step that she took as she tried to find her way out had been heavy, and she continued to sink lower and lower into the abysmal sea of fear, guilt, anger, misery, and, above all, pain. The pain was unbearable. But then she heard his stories. The voice that spoke to her became her own guiding light, but it was muddled, like sounds underwater. Its cadence and tone were all wrong, and she couldn't place who was speaking to her, not even if the voice was male or female. She just knew that it meant the world to her. It had soothed her to know she wasn't alone, and though she couldn't remember who it belonged to, she needed to get back to it.

I couldn't remember. I can't remember.

"Why can't I remember?"

Luke's rhythmic stroking stopped, and she realized then that she'd spoken out loud. He tilted his head back, and when she lifted her own, he wiped the tears from her eyes. "What's the last thing you remember?"

Johanna shook her head, but Luke cupped her cheeks. His touch was soft yet constant, reminding her that she wasn't alone. She just had to reach out, to try.

"It hurts. There's something affecting my memories, and when I try to remove it, it hurts."

His hand went into her hair again, smoothing it away from her face. "Then leave it. It might be there for a reason."

"But what reason—"

The grimace on his face silenced her. He knew something, and whatever it was, it was terrible.

"Luke did someone—"

His face grew tense as a haunted look invaded his eyes. Johanna squeezed his shoulders, hoping to ease whatever news he was about to share. He looked over her again before he said in a tight whisper, "You were almost dead when I found you."

Johanna gasped, her eyes growing wide.

"And you've been here, at my house, unconscious for the last two weeks." He took a deep breath, his face stoic. "During that time, we've only interacted through your abilities. You've gone from protecting this house and me, for a variety of reasons, to communicating with me on mental and energetic levels. So whatever is happening, you did it to protect yourself."

She shook her head rapidly. "No, no. I don't have the ability to create mental blocks. Those are higher level skills in my family—" Johanna yelped as another bolt of pain flew through her body, causing her to squeeze Luke's shoulders in a death grip.

"Johanna!" He gripped her arms, pulling her closer, holding her tighter.

She took a deep breath. As her grip eased, he instructed her to take another one, going so far as to take one with her. Slowly, ever so slowly, the pain went away. Only then did she look up at him, confused and shocked. "Is there some way to be sure that no one else did this to me?"

Luke nodded. "I called a witch that we've known for centuries. She can trace magic, and the only source she felt came from you." He rubbed the length of her spine as she fell against him, her body needing his for strength and support. They stayed like that for precious minutes before he asked, "What triggers the pain?"

Johanna's fingers slid down his sides, coming to rest at his back as she held onto him. She was scared that even the mention of what happened would trigger the pain, but she knew she had to share the information for him to help.

"When I try to remember what happened, or when I think of my ancestors." She braced herself but felt nothing. She sighed in relief, then cautiously turned over her next words in her head to pick ones that would hopefully not trigger the pain again. "My mental abilities are hereditary, like most witches, but I still don't know how I could have made this mental block."

Luke's arms tightened around her as she settled into his warmth. "Can you tell me what your powers are?"

"Telepathy, mind control, telekinesis, and teleportation."

"Teleportation?" Luke asked.

She nodded. "That's the hardest one to learn, but it is entirely possible." Johanna bit her lip, making a noise of disgust.

"What is it?" Luke continued to rub her back, the soothing motion making her feel safe enough to be honest.

"Those abilities were used to kill people in the past, even vampires. Because of that, I wasn't taught to master them," Johanna whispered.

Luke made a soft humming sound. "They probably deserved it. That may cause some complications with The Council later, but it doesn't cause any with me. How do you create a mental block?"

"It's extremely complicated. It needs a lot of practice and focus, but essentially an item is determined and a restriction is placed upon it. Whenever that person violates that restriction, a punishment occurs."

"Like your pain?"

"Yes. But I can't think of a reason why I would block out so much. The larger the block, the more energy it takes and the harder it is to break it."

Luke continued to rub her back, his fingers

caressing her skin as she snuggled closer into his embrace. She knew it was strange, but thus far all their interactions had been, and she didn't have the strength to fight against the comfort he made her feel.

Luke's voice was quiet, gentle, as he asked again, "What's the last thing you remember?"

Johanna closed her eyes, letting the lull of his heartbeat give her confidence as she tried to remember something, anything. "I was leaving the hospital after visiting … my grandmother!" She pulled back, beaming with excitement. "She'll know what to do if I just—"

Luke's face went from confusion, to horror, and then a blank sadness that infected her, squeezing her heart.

"Luke, what is it?" she asked shakily.

"Johanna," he said with a swallow, "your grandmother passed away six months ago."

And just like that, Johanna shattered all over again.

CHAPTER 10

Luke sighed and looked down at the golden angel pressed against his chest.

Last night had been a whirlwind. Johanna had been distraught at the news of her grandmother's death. The grief, the realization that she had lost six months of time and couldn't even try to remember anything about her family without feeling the backlash of her own abilities, and the information that she had been unconscious for weeks was too much for her to bear. She'd cried herself to sleep, and Luke didn't blame her. In his opinion, she was taking the news well. He couldn't imagine how it would feel to not have the support of people he loved and trusted around him, especially when he woke up in a strange place with someone he didn't know.

Then there was their mate bond. In the span of the few minutes she'd been awake, he'd nearly kissed her three times, and he was deeply aware that it wouldn't have stopped there. What was worse was he knew she wanted him as well. Mate bonds had different intensities and theirs was incredible, but he'd resist it or die trying. Luke wanted Johanna to feel comfortable with him, and while in her moment of grief she'd turned toward him and had desired him, he knew a lot of that may have been from the mate bond itself. He wanted her care, her love, and he was willing to fight through anything for her, even the need to take her and make her his. This wasn't the time for that. No, his mate needed someone to be there for her right now, and that's what he wanted to be: her confidant. He wanted her to trust him completely, and while fucking her into oblivion would be enjoyable, her possible regret afterwards would kill him.

And then there was his own fear and insecurity. Johanna had to rely on him until she got her memories back, and while he was sure that would foster some sort of feelings for him, would she choose him in the long run, especially after she remembered what happened to her? Luke wasn't sure of the torture she'd been through, but he had several concerning ideas—after all, she had blocked herself from remembering six months of trauma. But one day she would remember everything, and she might blame him in the same ways he blamed himself.

He looked down at her, his fingers sliding through her hair carefully, not wanting to wake her. Her chest rose and fell peacefully, her breathing long and deep. Her hand curled over his chest where she had been holding onto him, while her head rest on his shoulder. Her long legs bowed over one of his underneath the blanket they shared.

The sight of her in his arms restored a piece of his soul, but he still couldn't sleep. Instead, Luke remained her faithful protector, staying awake to watch over her. He didn't want to miss when she woke up, didn't want her to feel alone. An irrational piece of him was also scared that she wouldn't wake up, that somehow she might have locked herself in another mental battle that would keep her away for days, maybe months.

While vampires didn't need sleep, they did function better with it. Maybe once he closed his eyes and finally rested, he'd be able to make some sense out of this mess. But until then he'd wait, and wonder, and worry, and try to tell himself everything was fine. Because it would be fine, it had to be.

Hours later, after the sun began to filter through the pale curtains and slowly bathe the room in light, Johanna stirred. It was a mesmerizing thing to Luke. She flexed first, wiggling her toes ever so slightly. The hand over his heart clenched. Her heartbeat quickened as it breathed energy into her gorgeous body. She shifted again, ever so slightly, but this time it was her hips that moved, and Luke had to bite his lip to keep from moaning. Then she did it again, but a frown appeared on her face as if she was confused.

"Good morning to you too, sunflower," Luke said, his voice teasing and slightly husky.

Her eyes flew open so wide he laughed, and then her mouth flew into a little "O" shape that was far too tempting. Luke mourned when it fell into a frown and a sad expression took over her face. He pulled her closer and his heart beat a little faster, satisfaction coursing through his veins when she snuggled into his warmth.

"Hey, it's going to be okay," he murmured.

Gently, because he couldn't resist, he kissed her forehead while his fingers softly massaged the knots starting to form in her shoulders. "I was thinking, maybe I could call Greg and Dani. They might be able to help you with your amnesia."

Johanna sighed softly. "I don't know if that would help, plus…" She trailed off, stiffening in his embrace.

Luke tilted her chin up to make her meet his eyes. "You don't have to guard yourself ever again, especially not around me. Whatever you're feeling or thinking, I want to know. I'm not going to judge you."

She averted her eyes, a small blush tinting her cheeks before she settled back down, tucking her head under his chin. She didn't speak for a few moments, but then a soft whisper left her lips. "I'm scared of remembering. I don't know what happened to me to get me here, but I know there are some things I wouldn't want to relive again. To block out my grandmother's death and force myself through this grief all over again, means that whatever is tied to it is worse than what I'm feeling right now." Johanna shivered, so Luke pulled her closer. "I don't know if the people I ... love are safe, or if I'm missing other important details. I realize that b-but..."

"It's okay," Luke whispered back. "It's okay to be scared. What you're feeling is completely normal. Anyone would feel that way. No one's going to force you to remember anything. If I ask Greg and Dani for their help, the most they could do is try to track down your ... loved ones and at least make sure they're safe while you're healing." His hand slipped under her hair to rub the back of her neck until she melted into him. "You don't have to save everyone, sunflower, and you especially can't if you don't heal."

She was quiet for a while, and Luke's mind spun with ways to help her feel better about the situation. He was so deep into his thoughts that he almost missed her say, "Okay."

"Okay?" he repeated.

Johanna nodded against his chest. "Please call them. I'd like to try."

———

Luke leaned against the door frame with his arms crossed as he waited for Johanna to get ready. He was worried about her. It hurt him to see her in so much pain, and he hoped that his family would be able to help her.

She stepped out of the bathroom in one of his shirts tucked into a pair of shorts. Her hair was brushed over one shoulder, spiraling down the length of her body, and he had to take a deep breath when her eyes met his.

"I'm ready," she said with a small attempt at a smile, but the slight tremble to her wrist, the way her shoulders rose closer to the top of her head as she tensed her back, and each stiff step she took told Luke otherwise.

He stepped closer to her, and she tilted her head up to meet his gaze. Her eyes widened ever so slightly as he stepped into her space, but she didn't shy away from him.

"Can you trust me, just for a second?" Luke asked.

She nodded softly, so Luke cupped her cheek. As he did so, Johanna's eyes fluttered closed. Soft as a wisp, he trailed his fingers down over her jaw to her neck, until he fit the back of it in his hand and drew her to him. His other arm slid around her waist, and he held her. She was tall, Luke guessed somewhere around 5'10", but even so her head only came to his chest, right over his heart and exactly where it was supposed to be.

In no time at all the tenseness flew away from her body. He took it until she too held him in the embrace.

"Better?" he whispered into her hair.

She nodded again before taking a step away from him. "I'm sorry."

Luke captured her face in his hands, making her meet his gaze. "Don't be sorry. Don't ever be sorry for needing a shoulder to lean on. I know"—his voice grew softer—"I know that all of this is strange and new for you. I know that you don't know me, but that isn't going to stop me from being here for you. I want to be here for you, and I will be, anytime you need me. There's no shame in having someone you can lean on, is there?"

Tears gathered in Johanna's eyes, but she didn't let them fall. Instead she shook her head and cupped his hands, giving them a soft squeeze. "Thank you."

They stepped away from each other. Johanna wiped her eyes and tilted her head toward the door. "They'll be here in a couple of minutes. We should go."

"They can wait as long as we need them to," Luke huffed.

Johanna looked at him for a moment, and then she laughed. It was a small hiccup of a thing that seemed to surprise her as much as it did him. Then it grew louder. Her hands went to her eyes again as she wiped at them with the backs of her fingers. Luke cautiously wondered if she'd crossed over into hysteria, but then she asked through a fit of giggles, "Are you always this argumentative?"

His eyes widened and he snorted. "I am not argumentative," he said, looking away.

Johanna laughed again, and even though he was embarrassed, it made him smile. "We will have to work on that. Come on." She held her hand out to him, and for a moment Luke stood dumbstruck at the action.

We.

The simple word shot through his heart like lightning.

A worried look came over Johanna's face and she began to draw back her hand.

No!

Luke reached out and took her fingers in his, interlacing them with his own. She visibly relaxed and together they walked out of the bedroom.

The front door opened as they entered the living room, and in walked Greg and Dani, followed by Mya. Luke had to school his face to not show the surprise he felt at Mya's appearance. Luke wanted to rip her a new one for ignoring him, but he knew now wasn't the time. At least she was here, and that was all he could ask for.

Johanna said hello to each of them. Luke noticed that she called them by name, which only served to further his suspicions that Zachariah had started torturing Johanna after she had begun working for the firm. The group made small talk for a few minutes, but then the conversation grew quiet and the silence awkward.

Luke broke it first. "Can you explain what it is you want to do to Johanna?"

Dani nodded. "I communicate with elemental spirits, and they in turn let me utilize their powers for my needs. I believe that by using the elemental spirit of water, I will be able to look into your memories without forcing you to see them as well. That way I'll be able to see if your—"

"Loved ones," Luke interjected.

Dani nodded. "Loved ones are safe."

"It may also help us see what happened to you and maybe help you get an idea of how to retrieve your memories," Greg added.

"And you?" Johanna asked Mya.

"I'm here for moral support." Mya swallowed. "It's also possible you may have information I'm searching for." Her gaze moved to Luke. "But I also wanted to make sure the both of you were ... well."

"We'll talk after," Luke said, and Mya nodded in response.

"Do you have any questions?" Dani asked.

Johanna shook her head. "No. Just ... thank you all for doing this."

"Of course, and thank you for letting me try." Dani smiled, then turned to Greg. "Could you get me a bowl of water, honey?"

Greg walked into the kitchen and Dani turned her gaze to Luke as she approached the couch he and Johanna were sitting on. "Sorry, bud, but for this I'll need you to not touch Johanna, or else I might end up seeing your memories as well."

Luke hesitated, not wanting to move away from Johanna. While outwardly she seemed fine, her spine was so straight and tense that he was concerned it would break in half. He was beginning to realize this was something she did when she thought she needed to hide. She froze her expression and did everything she could to make herself invisible, to make those around her believe she wasn't a concern. Luke was familiar with the action because he'd been doing the same thing for the last six months, and he didn't like that his mate felt she needed to hide here, when she was safe with him. Whatever had made this a normal response for her had happened before Zachariah, before Johanna had ever come into Luke's life. Luke wanted to erase it, and while he knew he couldn't get rid of it in an instant, he could at least take the first step in trying.

Luke leaned forward, shocking Johanna into looking up at him. "I see you, Johanna. You don't have to be scared. I'm right here, and I will never let anything happen to you again," he whispered into her ear, low and quiet enough that even she would have to strain to hear him.

When he pulled away, her eyes were warmer. He squeezed her hand and she squeezed back before he scooted away.

While he knew Dani had not heard what he'd said to Johanna, he saw the smile that touched her face before she sat down. Greg carefully placed the bowl of water in Dani's outstretched hands, and she turned to Johanna, her voice soft, coaxing, as she spoke.

"We'll need to both take a sip of this, then run our hands through the water, and lay them on top of one another. I believe that will allow your power to accept my intrusion into your mind, and then I will look at your memories. You shouldn't feel anything while I do this, but if you do I want you to say something right away and I will pull out, okay?"

Johanna nodded. She took a deep breath and took the first sip of water, and then Dani followed. They both slipped their hands into the water, coating their skin with the liquid, and then sat cross legged on the couch, facing one another. Dani placed her hands on Johanna's lap, palms up, and instructed Johanna to clasp them with her own. Once she did, Dani said, "Close your eyes. My magic tends to feel like electricity, and since I'm working on you internally, you may feel small charges under your skin. But I promise I won't hurt you."

"I know," Johanna said softly.

A pressure released into the room, weighted enough to feel as if the humidity in their environment had changed, but of a soft quality, like steam hitting the skin. When Johanna spoke again, her voice had a strength to it that it had lacked before. "I allow you in, Daniella."

Dani smiled and closed her eyes. A static electricity blended into the humid pressure in the air, connecting with the surrounding moisture and firing small bolts around them. Luke watched the spectacle, as amazing as it was terrifying. Neither Dani nor Johanna seemed to move beyond a small tense here and there. Sometimes Dani's face fell into a frown, or Johanna's and Dani's arms twitched, but otherwise they were soundless, motionless.

Then Dani screamed.

Greg, Mya, and Luke were on their feet in an instant. The three watched as she yanked Johanna into her arms and cried, her sobs reverberating off the walls. Luke looked at Johanna, taking in the tears rolling down her cheeks that were at odds with the look in her eyes. She seemed confused, her brow in a frown even as the tears continued to pour from her.

Greg approached Dani, but the look she gave him, gave everyone in turn, was fierce. She pulled Johanna closer as if she was protecting her *from* them. Dani's message was clear and heartbreaking, and it told Luke everything he needed to know: Whatever had happened to Johanna was worse than he could have imagined, and it was possible that one day his mate would look at him with just as rage and damnation as Daniella did.

When they were finally able to pry Dani away from Johanna, Greg and Mya ushered her into the kitchen while Luke knelt at Johanna's feet.

"Sunflower," he murmured into her hair as he hugged her, "do you remember—"

"No! No, but I feel … everything." Johanna clung to him as he gently rubbed her back. "I don't remember anything, but I feel *so* much!"

Luke stayed quiet, waiting for Johanna to continue. He didn't understand what had just happened or what she was feeling, and because of that he didn't know how to fix it for her.

"Everything hurts," she mumbled into his neck. "All I feel is guilt. Every time I look at all of you, I feel so guilty and I don't know why. I don't know what I did, but I'm so sorry. I'm so, so sorry."

She pulled back, shaking her head. "I shouldn't be here, I should—"

"Don't *ever* say that again," Luke hissed, making Johanna's eyes widen. He squeezed her sides. "I want you here. I *need* you here. Whatever it is you're feeling, it's not from us."

"But—"

"You haven't done anything wrong, sunflower. I swear to you, you haven't." Gently, so very gently so that Johanna could pull away if she was uncomfortable, Luke cupped her cheeks. He wiped away her tears and leaned his forehead against her own. "Breathe with me."

Her eyes shut, and she took one slow, shuddering breath, then another. Little by little she relaxed against him. Luke pulled back, wiping at her eyes and cheeks once more until she looked up at him with eyes filled with sorrow.

"I do feel guilt," he said softly, and she bit her bottom lip, "but I don't feel guilty *because* of you. I feel guilty *for* you. I hate that you're here right now, feeling this way. I hate how much you've cried since you regained consciousness. I hate that you felt the need to protect yourself so much that you locked away your memories. You are the one person I should have been strong enough to protect and keep safe, and I didn't. And I'm not the only one who feels that way. We, everyone under this roof right now, feel that way about you. You deserved better than that, sunflower, and you still do."

Johanna made an indescribable noise, something between a groan and a whimper.

He wiped more of the wetness away from her skin. "You may have had to make choices that you didn't like, that under normal circumstances you would never have made. But your circumstances weren't normal, and no one here will ever blame you for whatever you did."

Johanna squeezed his hand. "Just because you won't blame me for it, doesn't mean I shouldn't be blamed."

"Well then, if we're going by that logic, do you blame me?"

"What?" She drew back, a snarl on her lips.

Luke had to fight back a smile at her reaction. "Do you blame me for not saving you?"

"Of course not," she huffed. "And you did save me. You're the reason I'm here today."

"Well then, if you can manage to not blame me when the whole reason you ended up in this mess is because you're my mate, then I think you can cut yourself a little slack, don't you?"

She shuddered in his arms, so Luke took hold of her chin, making her meet his eyes. He gazed into them, trying to convey the awe he felt for her and her strength, the pride he had in her. "You made choices to survive, Johanna, and I for one am happy you made those choices, because if you didn't survive, I would have gone with you."

Johanna gasped and tried to draw back, but he wouldn't let her. Fire raged in her blue orbs as she clasped onto his shirt and tried to shake him, but he wouldn't budge. His resistance only seemed to make her angrier.

"You can't say that," she hissed. "You can't say things like that. That's not right. You didn't even know me. You didn't even *love* me. You can't just up and toss away your life like that for me. I would've never allowed that."

Luke smiled and clasped her hands as he leaned into her, pushing them both back against the couch, but when he spoke his voice was a low growl. "Interesting you say that, little sunflower. Would you like to know how I found out you were my mate? The *exact* way you let me find out?"

"How?" she said between rapid breaths.

"You masked our mate bond for months. Months!" he bit out. "Every time I tried to talk to you, you ran away from me. Every time I showed an ounce of interest in you, you rejected me. For *months*. And then in the middle of a battle with my enemy you used your powers to hold me down while claiming it was to protect me. Then you left. You made me watch you leave with *him!*

You made me watch him drag you away from me, all because you wanted to save me. So do not tell me what I would and wouldn't do for you. Do not tell me that I have to love you to offer to save your life, to beg someone to take mine in place of yours, when you did it so easily. Love had nothing to do with it. Our mate bond and what could be between us one day was enough for you to make that choice, and it is enough for me every day, every fucking *second*, to decide to make that choice for *you*!"

"Luke, I'm sorry," she whimpered, and the sound made his blood boil hotter. She made a low, soft whine, and he watched as the fight left her. Her anger and righteousness morphed with his to form a single, sudden emotion: desire.

Johanna pulled at his shirt, dragging him closer, and he pinned her down against the back of the couch until there was no room between them. Her silky thighs hugged his waist as he grabbed her hips. She was so close, so fucking close, and he had hoped, dreamed, fucking prayed for this moment more times than he could count.

Her lips parted as his descended, coming achingly close, and then he heard a noise in the other room and everything came rushing back.

Luke sighed, clasping onto the back of the couch as he tried to remind himself that he couldn't act on the very real temptation in front of him.

Johanna's eyes opened and she whined. She rolled

her hips, but he held her still, and when she couldn't pull him to her, she huffed.

Luke had initially thought there was nothing sexier than having Johanna against him, but he was wrong. Seeing her want him just as much as he wanted her was a whole new high, and it was killing him to fight against it.

"Why?" she murmured.

Against his better judgment, he rested his head in the crook of her neck, felt her pulse pounding under her skin, and groaned.

She clawed at his back, trying to get him to satisfy the need rushing through her, but he resisted.

"I can't. Not yet, sunflower," he whispered against her skin.

"Why?" she demanded again.

"Because I would rather not traumatize my family with the sight of me thrusting into you, and I'd prefer to keep your screams to myself."

"Luke," she moaned, squirming in the chair, a blush falling over her pale skin all the way down to the tops of her breasts.

The scent of her desire grew heavier in the air. He took a deep breath, inhaling it. He could almost taste it on his tongue. And the sight of her, with her legs spread around him, hands on his chest, and her beautiful full breasts rising and falling with every short, rapid breath she took had him begging the gods for patience and strength. Luke had to force himself away from her *right now*, or else he would go back on everything he'd said and find out exactly how good her pussy would feel when it was milking his cock.

Finally he shifted, and Johanna's hands fell away as he stood. His voice was still thick and husky as he said, "I'm going to go find out what Dani saw. I'll be right back."

Johanna blinked sharply, as if he'd dumped cold water on her. Then she nodded, and Luke left while he still could.

CHAPTER 11

Luke entered his kitchen to see Dani huddled between Greg and Mya. Her red eyes met his and he sighed as he crossed the space to stand at the island in front of her.

Her eyes darted around and behind him before coming back to his face. "Where is she?"

"In the living room," Luke said.

Dani's voice cracked as she spoke. "How is she?"

"Confused." Luke reached across the table to squeeze Dani's hands. That they had stood so many times in this same position while she comforted him wasn't lost on Luke. In fact, it terrified him. It had been months since he'd seen Dani so shaken.

"Johanna is … struggling," he said finally. "Whatever the two of you did has forced her to feel things from the last few months. She still doesn't remember anything, but she's experiencing the emotions of those lost memories. Right now, the primary one is guilt. I've explained to her that there's no reason for her to feel that way, but I don't know what I'm fighting yet, Dani. What did you see?"

Dani looked to Greg, who nodded. She sniffled and rubbed her eyes before taking a deep breath and letting it out. "I could only see the surface level, there's … a lot under there that I can't access. I don't think it's safe to say his name around her right now." Her gaze touched each of them and Luke knew she meant Zachariah. "But we don't have to worry about him coming after her. That's the good news. I don't quite understand how, but I think she teleported to you."

Luke jerked back. "To me?"

"Yes. I don't know how her magic works—she's the only one who can answer that—but her desire was to see you. This house has the biggest concentration of your energy, so she came here. He doesn't know where she is. He doesn't know your address. At least, he never learned it from her, so she's safe here." Dani's eyes narrowed and she balled her hands into a fist. "But he will come after her, Luke. He enjoyed using her powers as a weapon, and he won't be willing to lose them."

A deep, animalistic growl came out of Luke. "Over my dead fucking body."

Dani took a deep breath. Greg squeezed her arm and Mya rubbed her back in comfort while Dani leveled him with a heartbreaking stare. "That's not the worst of the news. H-He raped her. Brutally. For sport. Every time we won, he took it out on her. Every single time. He *butchered* her. Those marks that were on her body when you found her were just from one day. He figured out how to use something similar to Mya's power to heal her so that we wouldn't see her wounds when she came to work. But he took his hatred of us out on her every chance he got."

Luke couldn't see, couldn't hear, couldn't feel anything besides rage. Insurmountable, undeniable, soul-binding rage that made him want to scream. He wanted to wage war, to tear the city apart until he found Zachariah and killed him and everyone that stood in between them with his bare hands.

Luke turned, looking for something, anything, to use as a weapon as he prepared for the fight of his life.

In an instant Mya was in front of him. "Luke! Stop!"

He went to push past her, but she refused to move. "Stop! Stop it, Luke. Don't do anything to scare her right now, please!"

But it wasn't Mya's voice that reached him, or Dani's or Greg's presence that shocked him still. It was Johanna's form standing in the kitchen. He took in her wide eyes and the sudden paleness of her skin, and he knew that she had heard everything. Instantaneously everything fled him and all he saw, all that mattered, was her.

Luke stalked over to her, but she put up a hand. He watched her erect that shield of hers, the one he had hoped she would never feel the need to use again.

"Sunflower—"

"It's okay, Luke," Johanna said in a level tone.

"It is *not* okay," he growled, grabbing hold of her arm and pulling her close to him.

She let him, but she didn't warm to his embrace or the nearness of his body like she had before. Instead she looked into his eyes, and he was chilled by the coldness in hers.

"It's okay for right now, then. I need to know what happened to me. I need those answers and I don't have time to react to them." Her gaze flickered and just a small bit of something warmer came through. Johanna whispered, soft enough so that even he could barely hear, "If you still want me after all of this, protect me then. But I need this now."

She pulled away from him and approached the island. "Please tell me everything you know, Daniella."

———

Johanna took a seat at the island. Her abilities as a mind witch allowed her to turn on and off different portions of her body, and to survive this she shut off her emotional epicenter: her heart. She could deal with her emotions later, but they had no place here.

Daniella, Greg, and Mya stood as a unit, carrying a pain that didn't belong to them. It belonged to Johanna and her alone. Seeing them like this was yet another reminder of why she couldn't stand to feel right now. They had one another to lean on, and it was evident that they loved each other dearly. She was the outcast here and this situation was all her own. No matter how welcoming they were, that was the truth. They could remember their pasts. They had not blocked out months of time and were not forcing themselves to play catch up. Not even twenty-four hours had passed since Johanna discovered how drastically her life had changed, and yet again she was forced to learn something so intimate, so horribly tragic and personal from a stranger.

Life had taught Johanna that respect was given to those who appeared to be strong and dependable, not weak and vulnerable. The world ate those souls up for breakfast. She believed more of the people in this room, even hoped one day she might be able to trust them with the pieces of her that she buried, but right now, in this very moment? No, now was not the time.

Johanna closed the last fissure of her heart just as Luke came up behind her, his warmth radiating into her skin. With one arm he leaned onto the counter, grasping the edge of it in his hand while he cupped her waist with the other. Even with her heart closed off, her body eased against his. Johanna squeezed his hand at her waist gently, a silent message of thanks before she focused back on Daniella.

"I heard everything you said to Luke," Johanna began, her voice unwavering. "Were you able to see anything else? Anything about my loved ones?"

Daniella sat up straighter at her tone. Her eyes were still red and watery, but not a single tear fell down her cheeks. "Not your immediate family, no. But I did see your grandmother." She took a deep breath as Johanna waited for her to continue. "He killed her in front of you."

Gasps and curses echoed around the room. Luke's hand clasped the countertop so tight Johanna thought she heard it crack.

Johanna gave a curt nod, and when she spoke again her voice was robotic, even to her. "Thank you for telling me. Did you see anything else?"

Daniella watched her for a moment, a question in her eyes, but then she shook her head. "No, that was all."

"Would you mind if we spoke alone?" Johanna said to Daniella.

Luke stiffened at her back, and she turned to look up at him. "It'll just be for a moment."

"I don't want to leave you," he said.

The look he gave her did something to her psyche. One of the bolts opened, the chain slipped out, and Johanna had to swallow hard as she was hit by a tidal wave of emotions. She breathed, squeezed his wrist, and said, "I'm fine."

His eyes narrowed at her words.

"I'll be fine. *Please.*"

"Luke, let's give them a second, alright? It's been a long day, and they both have some things they need to get off their chests," Greg said.

Mya nodded and made her way out of the room, but

Luke looked like he wanted to argue and Johanna knew he had so much more left to say. He stared into her eyes, and something there must have gotten through to him because he finally took a step away from her, and then another, and another.

As Luke left, he took something of hers. Her safety. Luke was the only semblance of comfort she had and without it, without *him*, there was something missing. Now she was left with this woman, someone who had seen so much more of her than she had ever wanted to show someone. It was terrifying.

Daniella's hands tentatively touched Johanna's, and she drew back at once, shock etched onto her face. Her chest felt tight and the air in the room seemed too thin. Daniella reached forward again, and this time Johanna had nowhere to go except to let Daniella touch her.

Daniella's fingers were soft and soothing on Johanna's own, and at the center of her palms Johanna's muscles began to relax. Slowly the feeling moved up her skin. With a gasp, Johanna realized that for the second time Daniella was doing something to help her, even when Johanna already owed her so much.

"T-Thank you," Johanna said.

Daniella gave her a small smile, then nodded to her side. "Why don't you come sit over here so we can talk privately. Vampires can hear ridiculously well, and I'm sure they're probably listening right now!"

There was scurrying in the background that would have made Johanna laugh in any other circumstance.

She moved to sit beside Daniella, and they turned to face one another, knees touching while their elbows rested on the island.

Once they'd settled, Daniella spoke. "'I'm sorry' doesn't even begin to describe how I feel for you, but I am. I am so incredibly sorry for what you went through."

"And I'm sorry you saw it," Johanna said softly.

"I'm not," Daniella replied, her voice stern. "We should have done better. We should have known *something*."

Johanna pressed her nails into her skin. "You can't blame yourself for that. Luke said I hid our mate bond. Between that and not being able to remember things about those I love the most, I don't think I would have let you."

Daniella touched her hand. "But why would you do that? You understand you're important, don't you?"

Johanna's smile was twisted and cruel, cut by misery and pain as she replied, "I'd say I'm not if this went on for six months and no one batted an eye."

Daniella winced.

"I don't blame you. I don't blame Greg or Mya, and I certainly don't blame Luke. But the fact is I'm one person in a crowd of a million people. If he did that to me, he did it to others too. The reason why it matters right now is because I'm Luke's mate."

"That's not true," Daniella hissed.

"Isn't it? If I was in such bad shape, weren't there

others who were worse? Did they make it out alive? Where are their heroes? Who misses them? Who comforts them? I got lucky," she said, spitting the bitter word from her tongue, "that's all."

The air grew hot between them. Daniella's spine lengthened as she sat up to her full height, and even though she was shorter than Johanna, she suddenly seemed so much taller, so much wiser. "They made it out alive," she said cuttingly.

"What?" Johanna said, her jaw falling open in shock.

"They made it out alive because you helped us save them."

Johanna shook her head rapidly. "I ... But ... I-I couldn't—"

"You shouldn't have, but you most certainly *did!* The last time Luke saw you, you saved his life. And when you saved his life and told him how to get to safety, you saved the lives of over eighty other enslaved immortals. If that wasn't enough, you also gave us the coordinates to several other locations where we've been able to rescue even more people and drive our enemy into a corner. So if you want to know who their hero is, it's *you.*"

Even though Daniella's voice was quiet, her words flayed Johanna all the way down to her bones. She was torn apart and reconstructed into something else all at once.

Daniella's eyes grew soft as she gathered Johanna in

her arms and held her. Her tears were silent but heavy with the weight of her sorrow, but Daniella never said a word to her. Instead, she rocked Johanna from side to side as she hummed a soft melody.

Slowly Johanna's tears stopped and Daniella, feeling the shift, released her. Johanna wiped at her eyes before Daniella handed her a box of tissues. Both of them looked at the box, then at one another, and laughed a laugh of those with a bond forged by indescribable trauma.

"I'm sorry for that," Johanna said.

"Don't be." Daniella sighed. "Honestly, I'm just happy I could be there for you."

"I can see why Luke likes you," Johanna said softly. Daniella was a beautiful woman, with springy dark brown curls that framed a heart-shaped face, kind brown eyes, and a stubborn tilt to her jaw. And yet her beauty went so much deeper than that. Johanna was in awe of her, and suddenly she felt so very shy and stupid in front of her.

Daniella hummed. "I wasn't always this way. Luke changes the people around him, whether you want to change or not. But it's always for the better."

Johanna nodded but averted her gaze.

"He likes you too, you know," Daniella said softly.

Johanna could feel her cheeks heat. While guilt had been the first emotion Johanna felt when it came to the missing six months of her life, there was another emotion she felt when it came to Daniella: envy.

She took a deep breath, wanting to clear the air while she still had the chance. "Did I … do anything to you? Before, I mean, in the last couple of months."

Daniella cocked her head to the side. "No, why?"

This is ridiculous. You were being ridiculous back then and you still are right now.

Johanna sighed. "I saw you and Luke together before all of this. The two of you were in an embrace. I know it was just a hug but … I was jealous of your relationship with him. That you could be that close to him. I think our enemy…" She gulped, swallowing back the emotions in her throat. "I think our enemy took me not too long after that, so I was worried that I had gone after you somehow."

Daniella bit her lip, and once Johanna finished, she laughed. A true, wholehearted, full belly-clenching laugh so alive, so infectious, that Johanna cracked a smile too.

"I'm sorry, I'm sorry just … Oh boy. Listen, I love Luke with all my heart, but like a brother. He's a great guy, one of the best I know, but he drives me way too crazy for that to ever happen." Daniella squeezed her arm. "Believe me, he's all yours, and I think the both of you know it too."

Johanna fidgeted but Daniella's smile only grew wider.

"Luke is my best friend, and I would really, *really* love to get to know the woman he's crazy about, if she doesn't mind."

A shy smile touched Johanna's lips, and she squeezed Daniella's hand. "I'd really love that."

"Good. Now, do you want to go see him?" Daniella asked.

Johanna tensed. "I-I don't know how he's going to see me after all of this. I'm worried he'll think I'm damaged goods," she whispered.

"He most certainly will not. Luke saw you. He's the one who brought you into his house and did what he could to make sure you held on until we got here. He's also the one who cleaned you up afterward."

"What?" Johanna said, covering her mouth.

"He wouldn't let anyone take care of you. Luke's been the only one watching over you the whole time you've been unconscious. While we didn't know where all your wounds were, he did, and I'm sure he had his suspicions about what caused them. But being suspicious is different to having the truth laid out in front of you. That's why he got so upset."

Johanna's hand fell to her lap. She opened her mouth to speak but found that she couldn't form the words.

"My point is that never changed how he treated you. If it didn't then, it wouldn't now. I know Luke well. I watched him, especially while we looked for you. You've been the only thing on his mind for a while now. That isn't going to go away because of the abuse you went through. If anything, Luke's going to be even more up your ass than he was before." Daniella squeezed her arm again. "Do you see yourself as damaged goods?"

Johanna thought over her question and then sighed. "It's hard not to. All of this is a lot, and it's going to take some time to process it."

"Then take that time. You're allowed to feel whatever you feel and have whatever thoughts you have. But feeling those things and having those thoughts doesn't make them true." Daniella sighed. "A few months ago, the monster that took you killed my friend."

Johanna gasped but Daniella continued. "He killed her because he couldn't get to me. In that moment I felt so guilty for being safe and alive and with a wonderful man who wanted me by his side. I felt like I robbed her of everything she could have had. And you know what Greg told me? That I shouldn't feel guilty for being alive. I could affect so many people's lives. In fact, I already had. He told me that I could do a lot of good by being here, and so can you. I'm not going to ask you to give Luke a chance, but I am going to ask you to give yourself a chance. Have you ever done that before?"

The answer was automatic, and a weight left her chest as Johanna whispered, "No."

"Well, maybe now's a good time to start."

CHAPTER 12

The room fell silent when Johanna and Daniella entered.

Johanna's eyes found Luke's immediately. She froze as everything else fell away. For a moment they just stared at one another, until Johanna noticed the little frown lines that stood out at the corner of his eyes and his now ruffled hair. Even his stance was different—tense and seemingly unmovable.

Is he even breathing? Am I?

She took a deep breath and watched his shoulders relax a fraction. Then it hit her all at once: he was worried about her.

Her heart softened. A second beat picked up under her skin, but it shattered at the clearing of a throat. When she came back to her senses, she realized she had been moving unconsciously toward Luke. Johanna looked away from him quickly, but not fast enough to miss the small, relieved smile on his face.

"We're going to head out for the day. Everyone needs their rest," Greg said.

"Thank you, everyone, for helping me," Johanna said.

Daniella nodded and then slipped her arms around Johanna in a hug. "I'll check on you in a bit, okay? Maybe we could get together later in the week and go shopping."

Greg groaned and Daniella shot him a glare. "Hush you."

Johanna smiled at their teasing. "I'd like that."

Before they left, Johanna pulled Mya aside. "I'm sorry I couldn't help you. But the second I remember something, I'll let you know. I promise. You'll find…"

Him.

Johanna drew back, unsure of why that word had come to her mind when Mya had never said what she was looking for.

At her hesitation, Mya stood straighter, hope warming her face. It was the first time she hadn't appeared devastated since the moment she'd entered Luke's home, and it made Johanna hesitate. But she couldn't give her false hope. Even if a part of her did know something, it, much like everything else, was locked away in her memories.

She cleared her throat and tried again. "You'll find what you're looking for."

Mya's shoulders dropped and she bobbed her head in a nod before filing out behind Dani and Greg.

Johanna was once again alone with Luke, but nothing felt the same. She was off balance, unsure of what to do, and to his credit he seemed to be in the same boat. Luke rested his head against the door, hand still on the knob, his body hunched over on the frame as if it was the only thing keeping him up.

She opened her mouth to speak, but words failed her and the fear that the ground had fallen out from underneath them was too thick for her to ignore.

Luke turned and marched toward her like a man ready for battle, only to stop a foot away. His eyes were so intense, full of a thousand different emotions, that they took Johanna's breath away. She realized then that he was afraid too, but not for the same reasons she was. His fear was out of respect. She could see it in his eyes, in the tenseness of his jaw as he ground his teeth together, in how his hand was frozen in mid-air as he resisted touching her. But Johanna's fear was out of self-loathing. That fear was rapidly forming a chasm between them, and if she didn't try to move past that feeling, it would only get wider.

Daniella's words repeated in her head. *Give yourself a chance.*

She took a step forward, closing the space between them. Their bodies swayed together, caught in each other's magnetism, but neither reached for one another.

Finally, Luke sighed, and the hand that had been hovering in the air caressed her cheek.

Johanna's eyes closed as she fought against the tears that threatened to spill out. One simple touch from Luke was all it took to decimate her heart. She wanted to tell him everything, every single horrible thought she had in that moment so he could see how messed up she was. She wanted to be vulnerable, to lay herself at his feet and show him all her broken pieces so he could decide if this was really the road he wanted to walk down, if she was really enough.

But the fact that he didn't pull her closer, didn't initiate any further contact except the whispering caress of his fingertips along her skin, told her that he knew. Somehow, he knew. He *noticed* her. Luke saw more than she willingly let on, and no matter how much she tried, she couldn't escape his gaze. And there was something so harrowing, so heartbreakingly glorious within that knowledge, that it sparked a tiny speck of courage which grew inside of her, urging her to open her eyes to meet his.

His breath hitched as he searched her gaze for something. Then, ever so softly, Luke whispered, "Stay with me."

She stared at him, confused. "How did you know?"

"Because I know what it's like to blame yourself for something and to wish things were different. I know what it's like to think you aren't enough and that you'll drag everyone else down if you let them in." His thumb grazed along her jaw as he said again, "Stay with me."

"And what if you change your mind?" Johanna said, averting her gaze.

"I won't," he replied without any hesitation.

"What if you do?"

Luke tilted her chin up, drawing her eyes back to his. "I would never do such a thing, but in the event there was ever something that affected the possibility of there being an 'us,' I would talk to you about it. That's what one does when they want to keep someone in their life. They fight for them."

His arm slid around her back, pushing her against his body, and even though his hold was light enough that she could leave, she didn't. Then he silenced every thought, every question she could have asked him.

"I still want you, sunflower. In fact, I'm beginning to think I've never wanted you more."

She crumbled. The floor fell out from under her, her knees buckled, and she fell into a heaping, sobbing mess. But Luke caught her, and she was starting to hope he always would.

———

Johanna leaned her head against the window, staring out into the backyard. The full moon shone, casting a blue light over every blade of grass and flower in Luke's garden. It was beautiful, but it could not pull her out of her thoughts. She was here, but not here. Seeing, but not focusing.

The rest of the day with Luke had been quiet. He comforted her while she remained silent. It wasn't that she didn't want to talk about what she was feeling—she did, but she'd been stuck on where to begin, what she could say that wouldn't scare him away but would help Luke to understand why she was like this now.

He'd given her time and taken care of her. She'd found out about the food he'd kept for her, but it had only reminded her of how much he had done for her, how much he cared. It both helped and hurt her, leaving her feeling that he had drawn the short end of the stick. But she couldn't tell him that, because she knew if she did, he'd convince her otherwise. Even in the short time since she'd awoken, she knew that's what he would do. Much like he'd said earlier, he'd fight for her. The question was, did she deserve to be fought for? And who fought on Luke's behalf? She wanted to fight for him, and that added a new level of depth and confusion to her already endless feelings.

She'd taken the feelings to bed with her and woken up shortly after, choking on a scream, so here she sat, procrastinating what she knew she'd have to do. She couldn't keep going like this. Even she knew that forcing herself to do a deep dive into her emotions wasn't healthy, but the alternative was worse. She couldn't keep crying. She couldn't move on from her thoughts, she couldn't sleep, she barely wanted to eat, and she couldn't possibly make a good, conscious decision when she was so utterly terrified of *everything* she did.

Johanna took a deep breath As she released it, she fastened back on her emotional chains, secured the locks, turned everything off, and then approached things one by one: shame, guilt, the expectations she had laid upon herself, sadness, anger, hatred.

Johanna heard a noise and turned her head just as the door creeped open. In it stood Luke. Everything about him made her feel safe. He was tall, probably 6'5" or 6'6", his shoulders were broad, and he was a solid wall of muscle. His presence, his *persistence*, shook her. It made her feel lucky, honored, feelings she wasn't used to. Now, though, she felt like running both toward and away from him.

He seemed to know that. She really didn't understand how, but once again he understood her.

Luke entered the room slowly, watching her every move. Finally, he said. "Couldn't sleep?"

Johanna shook her head and curled herself more into a ball against the wall.

"May I?" He gestured to the other end of the window seat, and she nodded again.

Luke moved toward Johanna like a lion whose cage had been opened—wary if what he could see was real, but courageous enough to find out. He sat down, his back against the wall, mirroring her stance while he propped one foot on the cushion and left the other on the floor. Then he held out his hand to her.

She was startled at first, but then she looked from his hand up into his eyes. There were no questions there, no doubt or fear, nothing but absolute certainty. And that certainty, that assurance that he had in not only her but in them had her closing her fingers around his and allowing herself to be drawn into his lap.

Johanna rested her head against his chest, peering out of the window while he wrapped his arms around her. She clasped onto his arm with both of hers. With a simple embrace he had separated her from the scared scrap of a being she had been. Now she felt at peace. Treasured. At home.

Luke didn't say anything, and neither did she for a while. They simply were. Then something in her changed, and she realized this was how she wanted them to be. She desired this, *craved* this, but she couldn't keep it if she didn't let go of the ugly monster in her heart.

"I wish we would have been like this before," Johanna said, eyes fixed on the moon-bathed garden.

"So do I," Luke said, and they both sighed.

"Luke, I..." Johanna took a deep breath and fitted herself closer, snuggling into his warmth. "I'm scared to tell you about what I've gone through before, but I know I have to if I want you to understand me and why I'm like this. Can I?"

He kissed her head. "You can always talk to me

about anything you want. I want to get to know you, sunflower, and it means a lot to me that you're willing to let me."

A retort started to form in Johanna mind, telling her that he wouldn't want to hear this story, but she bit it back. Taking another deep breath, she began.

"I lived in a small town as a child. I was a big girl, even at that age, and that made me the butt of every joke and bullied by everyone: boys and girls, even their parents."

Luke tightened his arms around her.

"It hurt. They weren't just cruel to me, but also to my loved ones. They assumed that they were neglectful of me and my health since I was the only one like this." Johanna waved her hand over her body. "I never fought them. I never said anything. I remember some people stood up for me at first, but as time went on and we all grew up it became just me on my own."

Luke's hand moved along her back, trying to erase the tension in her spine.

"I let in anyone who wanted to be a part of my life. I dedicated myself to them. I thought having someone was better than having no one, and it didn't matter if they only kept me around because I fulfilled a need for them, or that I was a second option. I just ... I didn't want to feel alone anymore. That continued through college. There, I..."

She swallowed hard, trying to fight back the anxiety clawing at her throat. Luke's arms tightened around her, reminding her that she wasn't alone, that she didn't need to drown in her memories.

She breathed, then whispered, "I was … sexually assaulted by the man I was dating."

"What?" Luke said, his arms tightening even more.

"Luke—"

"Who was it, Johanna?"

She could feel him shaking around her, and when she looked into his eyes, they were red, furious. "Luke, you can't hurt him," she said gently, squeezing his arm.

"Like hell I can't. Give me his name, Johanna, right now."

She smiled despite the memory and his murderous intent. "Luke, as a vampire you're forbidden from killing humans, remember?"

"He hurt *you*," Luke hissed.

Johanna brushed her fingers over his cheek. "He did, but I took care of it."

"What?"

"If you let me finish my story, I'll tell you how."

Johanna watched him weigh his options. His muscles were still tense and his eyes still bright red, so she knew she hadn't convinced him to let this go.

"I wouldn't want anything to happen to you, especially not because of me," Johanna whispered as she caressed his skin. "Please."

Luke rested his head back against the wall and blew out a harsh breath. With it, some of the tension left his body and when he looked at her again, his eyes were almost back to normal.

"Thank you."

Luke grunted in response. Johanna rested her head under his, but this time she wrapped her arms around his back. He sighed and hugged her. It was a little too tight, but she wouldn't complain.

"I left college after that. I was too ashamed to tell my loved ones what happened. Soon after, my grandmother got sick. The closest hospital was in New York so I decided to move here to spend as much time with her as I could. Everyone thought it was a horrible idea. You need to be tough to make it out here, you need to have a backbone. You need to be a fighter, and I'd never shown any promise in those areas."

Luke huffed but otherwise stayed silent.

"At first, they were right. It was hard being here essentially on my own. But this was my chance at a fresh start away from all the horrible experiences I'd had back home. No one knew me here, and so I could be anything, anyone, I wanted to be. My grandmother was also a formidable woman. She was a child during one of our wars, and she believed if you were backed into a corner, you should always fight to get yourself out."

"She sounds like a wonderful woman," Luke said, relaxing a little more under her.

"She was. You would have loved her. She was good for me, and the city was good for me too. But then I found out the man from college had taken pictures and a video of me the night he'd assaulted me."

Luke tensed again and she could tell he was going to say something, so she cut him off before he could. "I took him to court. When the case seemed like it wasn't going in my favor, I forced it to. I manipulated the judge with my powers, and I took revenge on the man who assaulted me. He's in a mental hospital right now, and he will never, *ever* get out."

"Good," Luke said firmly.

"That's not *good*, Luke!" She tried to draw back from him but he wouldn't let her. "That's not something someone should do. That's not something a *good* person would do. I broke him, and I enjoyed it. I was *proud* of it! I went on with my life. I had no remorse back then, but now I find out that it happened all over again and I dragged my grandmother into it. She died because of *me!* What if that's my penance? What if all of that was just karmic justice for what I'd done? What happens if I do it again and I draw someone else into it, like you? I'm not … I'm not worth it, Luke. I'm just not."

Luke brushed her hair back from her face. "So that's what you're scared of?"

A little part of Johanna shriveled and died as she nodded.

"Sunflower, no one deserves what happened to you."

She shook her head.

"Do you think I'm a good person?" he asked.

She sighed. "Of course you are."

Luke's lips tipped up at her response. "I've killed people. A lot of people."

"And I'm sure you did it for a reason."

"So what's the difference between me and you?"

Johanna threw her arms in the air. "I was selfish, Luke! I did it because I was angry and I wanted justice."

"The difference between being called the hero or the villain is the person telling the story," Luke said.

"I don't understand what you mean."

"It's simple. You think you're the villain because you took revenge, but you're not. Against all the odds, you took what happened to you and let it go. You moved on with your life until it escalated, and when you tried to get justice for yourself and thought you wouldn't, you made sure you did. You call that being selfish, but you don't know who else that person assaulted. By getting away with it once, they could have done it a hundred other times. They could have been planning to do it again the night they won the case. You don't know what could have happened, but you stopped whatever it was from happening. That makes you good, Johanna."

She shook her head, but he cupped her cheeks to make her focus on him.

"You're good, sunflower. And as for what happened to you and your grandmother, I don't think karma had anything to do with that. I think..." He paused seeming to search for the words.

Johanna gripped his wrists in desperation. "Please, tell me."

"I think the reason you went through all of this is because you had the strength to."

Johanna's eyes widened.

"I need you understand that doesn't mean I think you deserved *any* of what happened to you. You don't, and the fact that you thought you did breaks my heart." Luke's fingertips rubbed over her cheek. "He took you because of who you are, and he kept you because of what you can do. But you beat him, sunflower. You saved people. You've continued to save people, and that's just from what we know now. Imagine what else we'll find out once you get your memories back. You took a horrible situation and did something good with it. Most people wouldn't be able to do that. Most people would have sacrificed everyone else over themselves. You did the complete opposite. You're a hero to those people, and every time you treat yourself like the villain you are trivializing what they went through. I know you don't want to do that."

She shook her head. "I don't, but I don't know how—"

"I understand how you were treated, and I understand why you think so poorly of yourself, but are those people around you right now?"

"No."

"Then why the fuck should their opinions matter?"

Johanna stared at him in shock.

"Every time you undervalue yourself, you let them win. Every. Single. Time. Meanwhile those people are off living their poor excuses of lives. Do you think they ever think of you, that you ever cross their minds? No. They've probably done that to a hundred other people by now. Does it seem fair to you that you're stuck while they're moving on?"

"N-No." She gulped. "But how can I change that?"

"Focus on you," he said quietly. "Think about what you want, every single day. I'm going to ask you and I want you to answer me as honestly as you possibly can. You need to learn how to put yourself first and that you don't need to sacrifice yourself for anyone else." His fingers brushed through her hair, squeezing her back. "You're allowed to do that, sunflower. Your words, thoughts and opinions have value. *You* have value."

She was shaking, bits of her heart exploding at his words. Logically she knew he was right, and if the roles had been reversed then she would have said the same things to him. Yet she never imagined she'd ever hear them come out of another person's mouth.

Johanna clung to him. She wrapped her arms around him and buried her head in his neck where she breathed in his scent.

"Would you do something for me?" Luke asked suddenly.

Johanna lifted her head. "Anything. What is it?"

"You spoke to me telepathically once. When you do that, can you only hear someone's communicative thoughts, or can you interact with all their thoughts?"

"Either or." She tilted her head to the side. "Why are you asking?"

"I want you to do that with me. I want you to see all my thoughts about you."

She drew back. "What are you talking about? Why would you want that?"

"Because I don't want you to ever doubt the way I see you."

"Luke…"

He squeezed her waist. "Please?"

"I … Okay."

He pulled her as close as he could, until she had no choice but to straddle his lap to accommodate them. Luke widened his legs, forcing her to spread her knees further and settle more onto his lap. She gasped, and goosebumps broke out across her skin when he chuckled slowly.

She took a breath, trying to slow her racing heart. "You know we don't have to be this close."

He smiled and tilted his head to hers. For a moment Johanna thought he was going to kiss her, but he rested his forehead against her own and stared into her eyes. "The last time we did this I couldn't reach you, so I don't want any space between us now."

She gulped and licked her suddenly dry lips. Then she closed her eyes in the hope of blocking out the intensity of his stare, but she could still feel him watching her. She blushed. "Close your eyes."

He laughed, the rumble of the sound making his chest brush against hers just as each puff of air tickled her lips.

Taking a deep breath, she gently pushed into his mind, feeling him resist her for all of a second. Then she was in.

The mind reflected a person's behaviors, so every mind was different. While Johanna was typically respectful of entering a person's mind, she enjoyed being able to see them for what they were. But Luke's mind had to be one of the most glorious she'd ever come across.

It was like a gallery, with blotches of paint and short form notes spilled along the marble walls and floors. Golden columns lined every archway, and when Johanna looked up, she could see an open sky-like field filled with countless shapes. Then she saw him. He looked into her eyes and everything changed.

The hall shifted, flying away until it was fully replaced with suns, the large, gleaming balls of light surrounding them. A giant bird flew in and out of focus before settling on the top of a cage covered in flames.

"This is how I see you," Luke said. *"To me, you are the sun. But you're also this bird, learning how to fly in a world that tried to tear you apart."* He reached his hand out and pointed at the bird. *"You'll learn how to fly, sunflower. This world could never keep you down. I won't let it."*

"Luke…" she said out loud, swimming in the mess he was making of her.

"Do you know why I call you sunflower?"

"No," she whimpered, opening her eyes.

"Because you are resilient. You persevere. You're strong, courageous, a beacon of hope." His hand slid from her waist up her side, tracing along her body. His fingertips lightly grazed the side of her breast, causing her to bite back a moan.

Johanna gripped his shoulders, her voice breathless as she said, "Luke, what are you doing to me?"

"Letting you know how beautiful I think you are, how utterly *desirable* you are to me." He released a sharp breath as he grabbed a hold of her hips and pulled her forward. She rocked against him, and they both moaned.

"I am over seven hundred years old, Johanna, from a time when women who looked like you would have been treated correctly, like a fucking blessing. Society is only obsessed with being thin now because of food scarcity and a million other things my brain can't focus on because I'm near you. But I can tell you that not a single one of them is true. The word 'fat' has a negative connotation to it, but that's not what it means, and it damn sure doesn't mean you're ugly, unintelligent, unhealthy, nor anything else anyone has ever called you. If you ever doubt that, feel free to look through my thoughts and I'll show you everything I've dreamt of doing to you since I first laid eyes on you."

She grew wetter with every word. Her nipples had turned into hard peaks, so sensitive that even the light rubbing of her nightgown as she panted was too much. Her body shook with need and want, but there was more than just desire coursing through her veins. Johanna felt vulnerable. Luke had turned her into fragmented chaos. Her soul begged for him to pluck her strings like an instrument and play her to whatever tune he wanted, just as long as he played her, as long as he touched her. Luke's honesty had flayed her open in such a way that she didn't want to ever be closed again. No, she wanted him to fill her empty spaces until every breath, every cell of her body had tasted his. And just as he had assured her, she wanted to assure him of where she stood, of what she wanted from him.

"I..." She took a deep breath to steady her nerves. "It's not only my loved ones that I don't remember."

He tilted his head, confused.

"It's you. I don't remember you. I protected the people I love ... and the person I knew I could fall in love with." She stared into his eyes, and a pop of satisfaction settled into her heart at his shock. "When I was unconscious, I heard you. I didn't know it was you at the time, but you're the reason I woke up. You made me feel safe. You made me feel comfortable, like I could trust you, like I ... had a home in you."

Johanna rubbed his chest, right over his pounding heart. "I want that home, Luke. I want you, and I'm willing to do whatever it is I need to do to be that for you. I want to be someone you can trust and confide in, someone that one day you can love."

His breath rushed out of him with a hiss, then grew shallow as he panted. Luke closed his eyes and tilted his head back, appearing tortured. A low, rumbling growl spilled out of his throat as he gripped the window seat hard enough to break it.

"Luke?" She reached out for him, gently caressing the side of his neck. His pulse thundered against her fingers so strongly she was concerned he was going to have a heart attack.

"I should have picked a different name for you, something wicked and dangerous," he murmured.

"What?"

His eyes opened, the darkness within them making her gasp. "You cannot say that to a man and then expect him not to struggle with losing control."

She blinked, then her mouth formed an "O" as she realized what he meant. His confession made her feel powerful, and with a soft giggle she started to get off his lap, but he pulled her back down.

"Absolutely not." His fingers flexed around her hips and a shiver traveled along her spine. "Stay, I just need a second to calm down."

She was still smiling as she nodded and rested her head in the crook of his neck. Every breath he took pushed at her chest and she took one with him, needing to settle herself as well.

Then he whispered, "I don't think you're going to have to wait very long."

"Hmm?"

"For me to fall in love with you."

CHAPTER 13

Johanna and Luke had spent most of every day of the last month together. She couldn't remember ever laughing as much as she had in her time with him, nor feeling as warm and cared for as he made her feel. They ate together, and no matter how busy Luke got, he always stopped to cuddle and sleep with her. When Luke wasn't with her, he was off being a busybody, flitting around doing something to what he liked to call "their" house, or working for the firm. Then Daniella announced she was pregnant, and he added worrying over her to that list. It was adorable.

There was really only one problem with all of this. Multiple times a day he asked her what she wanted, as a way to remind her to check in with herself. As the days went on and he kept asking her that question, she kept having to stop herself from saying "you."

Sometimes she thought he knew. The side of his lip

would curl into a smirk, and she swore he almost dared her with her eyes to say it, but she never did. She didn't know how to yet. Yes, she felt like she was healing quickly—due to having such a positive and caring environment around her with someone who treated her well, and her growing friendship with Daniella—but at the end of the day she still didn't feel as worthy as she now knew she should.

So, much like Luke, she kept herself busy when he worked. Johanna had started looking the roster of employee IDs, hoping to find more coordinates, but it was difficult. While she had clearly been the one to come up with the code, it was like looking at someone else's handiwork. The her that had made these had been in an entirely different mental space. She had been efficient, powerful, *desperate*. She wanted to save as many people as she could, and it was hard to be forced to see herself the same way Luke and the others saw her.

What she had done was incredible and compared to the way she saw herself now, it felt like she'd taken ten steps back in time. Every time she thought she might have figured out part of her code, doubt crept over her and caused her to second-guess herself. It was important that when she determined a new location, it was correct. If not, she could very well be sending everyone on a wild goose chase or, if she wasn't careful, into a trap. She was playing with people's lives, so she had to do this correctly. Luke, Daniella, Greg, and even Mya were counting on her and she didn't want to let them down.

She sighed, raking her fingers through her hair as she leaned her elbows on the table. She stayed like that as she heard Luke step into the room.

"Hey," he said, dropping a kiss on her forehead. "Having a tough time?"

She looked up at him. "Yes. I just have no idea what I was thinking when I made these. I can't get into that headspace to figure any of this out."

He frowned as he sat down next to her. "I wouldn't want you to get into that headspace. You were being held captive and I don't think you believed you were going to make it out alive. I'd rather you feel comfortable now and never figure these out than feel that way again."

She slumped in the chair. "I swear, did you write the book on smooth talking and how to be a Casanova? I can never win with you."

He laughed so deeply it brought a smile to her face. "What can I say? You bring out the best in me."

"Charmer."

Luke pulled her into his lap and she came easily, wrapping her arms around him. "How would you feel about taking a break?"

"A break?" She tilted her head to the side. "What do you mean?"

"I would like to take you out on a date. I thought we

could take my bike down to the beach, have a nice dinner, maybe dance a little. It would be good for us."

She sighed as the warmth of his gesture ran through her. "But can we really go out? What about—"

"We'll be fine." He kissed her head again. "I know the area well. It would be odd for him, or anyone against us, for that matter, to be out there. Plus, there's also a couple of immortals I know who like to frequent the restaurant. They'll help us if we need it."

Johanna released a breath, letting it carry the tension out of her body before she looked up at him and smiled. "Then I'd really love to go with you. I'll go get ready."

She kissed his cheek and caught the wide grin on his face before she wriggled off his lap and went to get dressed.

———

Johanna had never been on the back of a bike before and wasn't quite sure what to expect, but the moment Luke took off she knew she'd never be the same. The feeling of the wind blowing around her as they sped off was exhilarating. She felt free, as if nothing and no one could hold her back. The purr of the machine between her legs was exciting, and the intimacy of holding on to Luke's back while he sat in between her legs, guiding the bike down the road, wasn't lost on her.

Johanna knew motorcycle riding could be dangerous, but she trusted Luke. Her body naturally understood what to do every time he took a turn, and he was careful with her, never going too fast, stopping too short, or cutting any corners. Like with everything else he'd done since she'd woken up in his house, Luke kept her care in mind, and it was making her libido jump off the charts.

By the time they got to the beach her legs were so wobbly she'd nearly fallen when she tried to get off the bike. Luke caught her with an arm around her waist and asked her if she was okay. She said yes, but she wanted to pummel him when she saw that damn smirk on his face. He knew! He freaking knew *and* he was amused by her reaction to him. The jerk!

Still, as they walked down the beach, listening to the waves crash against the shore and the soft laughter of children surrounding them, she felt at peace. Looking up at Luke, she smiled. "Thank you for bringing me here. It's really nice."

His features softened with his own smile, and he wrapped his arm around her shoulders, falling into step beside her. "The smile on your face is thanks enough."

She laughed at him. "You're such a sap."

"You love it."

"I do," she agreed, the words slipping out of her mouth. For a second, she thought to backtrack, until she turned and saw that Luke was frozen in shock like a giant, handsome statue. Laughter spilled from her at the sight, and before she knew what was happening, he picked her up and threw her over his shoulder. Johanna laughed even harder, wiggling and yelling at him to put her down.

"Not a chance in hell. I cannot believe you, teasing me like that," he said gruffly.

"Oh my god! Are you *blushing?*"

Luke made a noise in his throat that set her into a whole new fit of giggles, and then his hand landed on her ass with a loud *whack!*

"Luke! No you did not!"

"I did, and, actually, I'll do it again." He smacked her ass again, and then he gripped her flesh, kneading it in his large palms.

"Luke, people can see!" she hissed.

He shrugged his shoulders under her, making her bounce. "Sounds like a them problem."

"You're impossible!"

"Yes, but now that I know you love it, why would I try to be anything else?"

———

Johanna heard the restaurant before she saw it, but then the two-story establishment covered in chipped blue paint came into view. It felt homey, with its waves of patrons, clinks of utensils, and laughter bouncing off the walls.

The staff smiled at her and Luke and welcomed them both warmly, but none more so than two of Luke's friends. Tommy, a werewolf, and Loe, a faerie, slid into their booth with them. Luke kept Johanna by his side and slung an arm over her shoulders while he introduced her as his mate. There was no hesitation in his voice, no hint of question. Even she caught the pride in his words, and she noticed his friends saw it too.

After hearing her darkest secrets, living with her for over a month, taking care of her, providing for her, and spending time with her, Luke seemed overjoyed about her being his mate. He'd said as much so many times she'd lost count, but it was one thing to say it behind closed doors and another to show it publicly. The weight of his conviction shocked her. It forced Johanna to finally question why she couldn't let go of her own self-doubt, and the answer was because she feared what would happen when she did.

But now, in this moment, she didn't want to be scared. She didn't want to have any of the fear, doubt, shame, or self-criticism she fought with daily. No, now she just wanted to be Johanna, Luke's mate. She wanted to listen to the way his friends made fun of him and the stories they told. She wanted to hear him laugh, let the warmth of his body seep into her pores ... so she did.

Eventually Tommy and Loe left to give Johanna and Luke privacy, and the evening gave way to eating, talking, laughing and teasing. Later, when she was full of good food and company, Luke twirled her in his arms in a darkened corner of the room and danced with her. Johanna couldn't remember the last time she danced, and she was grateful that Luke had made sure to keep the moment private between them. Like normal, he seemed to just sense her, to know her without her saying a word or sharing her thoughts with him. It felt so good to be so in tune with someone.

Luke's eyes flickered away from hers for a moment before he said, "The sun's setting. Why don't we go out to the pier and watch it together before we head home?"

Johanna nodded. The sun had been a long way from setting when they had stepped into the bar, but it was easy to lose track of time when she was with him.

"Let me go use the restroom," she said, squeezing his hand before separating from him.

"I'll wait for you at the entrance."

Johanna stared at herself in the bathroom mirror, taking in the person she saw. Her cheeks were rounder and fuller than she remembered, but high. Smile lines had started to form around her mouth, and her eyes twinkled back at her with joy and mirth. She looked younger, more at ease, as if life had been good to her.

It hadn't, she knew that, but when she tried, she couldn't recall all the moments she used to hold on to with a vice grip because *some* life was better than *none*. Now she felt grateful, because the person staring back at her was someone she'd always hoped she could be but had lost faith would ever appear. For the first time in her life, Johanna was starting to love herself, to care more about who she was and to believe she could do anything she put her mind to.

She awoke each day with an open heart, and at the core of it were the feelings she kept for Luke. Maybe tonight she'd be honest and tell him. He deserved to know, after not only helping her to start the chain reaction that was guiding her down the path of who she wanted to be, but for also nurturing and protecting her while she traveled it.

With new resolve, she dried her hands and opened the bathroom door. She was on her way to the entrance when a rowdy man tumbled into her path, causing her to jump backward to avoid running into him.

"Fuck off, all of ya!" he said, his voice slurring as he mumbled.

"Excuse me," Johanna said as he blocked her own path to the outside.

"Ah, look what we have here." He tried to smile but it came out crooked. "Come on, pretty lady, dance with me."

"No, thank you. Excuse me. I'd like to leave."

His laughter was interrupted by a hiccup. He stepped closer to her, so Johanna stepped away.

"Like to leave with me, huh?" he said with a drunken wink.

Johanna had to restrain her temper. She was utterly disgusted by his words, but this man was clearly an angry drunk and she didn't want to make him more upset or cause an issue, so she forced herself to be polite. "No. Please get out of my way."

"Oh!" he said in a sing-song voice. "She thinks she's too good for me, huh? Now listen here, you fat bitch—"

"Is there a reason," a voice started behind her, low and deadly, "that you're harassing my wife?"

Luke's arm wrapped around her, and Johanna's back straightened against his chest.

"Hey, m-man," he stuttered, slurring his words as he held up his hands. "I'm n-not causing any trouble. But this broad here—"

"My wife, you mean?" Luke snarled, the rumble in his chest vibrating against her back.

"Yeah, yeah, your girl or whatever—"

"Luke," Johanna said to him telepathically, but he didn't answer her. She wanted to turn to look at him, to see if that would make him refocus onto her, but some-thing in her told her not to. Luke wasn't thinking with the mind of a human right now; he was solely a predator protecting what was his.

"Luke," she tried again, ignoring the man's voice.

When Luke still didn't respond, Johanna ran her palm down the arm around her waist. She clasped his fingers, and he squeezed her stomach, hard. It was a warning, but she didn't care. If she didn't stop him, he'd do something that would get him in trouble with The Council. There were too many humans here for him to become violent, and as she looked around the restau-rant, she could see people on their cell phones. If Luke did *anything* supernatural, those devices would turn on them in a heartbeat.

"Luke! You can't. Please, let it go!"

The only answer she received back was a growl.

"—yeah, you know man, bitches can't be trusted," the man, clearly unaware of how close he was to his own death, said with a shrug and a sly grin, as if he was winning a game.

Behind her, Luke buried his lips in her hair, parting the strands. He kissed her head but then she felt the sharpness of his fangs as he grinned against her scalp.

Fuck.

"I'm sorry, Luke, but I can't let you get in trouble for me."

Johanna used her power to freeze his body in place. The ease and speed of which her ability worked surprised her, but she didn't have time for the shock. She refocused, making sure not to put Luke under full paralysis. He could still hear and experience his surroundings, but he would not be able to move.

She closed their telepathic connection. Johanna didn't want to hear what she assumed would be curses and demands for her to let him go, but even with that closure she felt his anger, and it was now directed at her.

So be it.

She took his anger and let it meld with her own. Together they created a dark explosion that flew through her veins and ignited her resolve. She looked at the man. "Shut up—"

He balled his hands into fists. "Now you listen here—"

"No, *you* listen!" Johanna hissed. "When a woman says no, she means no! How many times does someone have to say that for you to get it through your fucking head? What do you think you are, God's gift to the female race?"

He laughed in her face. "Oh you've got a mouth on you. Has your man never taught you how to use it right? I'm sure you could keep him a lot longer if you learned how to shut up."

Her eyes narrowed and she smirked. "And I'm sure if you knew what to do with your mouth you wouldn't be here drunk, alone, and stumbling over your own two feet."

"You bitch—"

Johanna was tired. For just one night, one *fucking* night, she didn't want anything to get in the way. Not her endless list of issues and criticisms, not her past experiences, nothing. And it had worked, she had *made* it work, and they were having a great night! But now this incredibly self-entitled piece of shit had ruined everything, and she fucking refused to let this continue.

It was easy to get into his mind. He had zero defenses, and with the liquor coursing through his veins he was a fucking mess. Still, she wasn't gentle about it, making it hurt as she slipped herself in. The mind was a map of chaos to someone not familiar with it, but Johanna *lived* here. The mind, even if it belonged to another person, was her home, so it was simple to find the place she was looking for: the faculties for relieving the bowels and bladder. All it took was a gentle push, and then she was out just as quickly as she'd slipped in.

Her grin grew into a small laugh. "Never mind. Even if you knew what to do with your mouth, no one would ever, *ever* want a man who smells like shit and can't even hold his own piss."

Horror dawned his face. He looked down, watching the wetness spreading over his pants. His eyes widened, and then he was running past Johanna and Luke and into the male stalls.

Johanna laughed again, a full body laugh that had her bending forward and then back as she rocked on her heels. But when she brushed against Luke's still frozen form, she paused. The victory that pumped through her died, because while she'd saved the man's life, Luke definitely wasn't going to be happy.

Instead of being timid, Johanna tilted her head up to his and pulled her magic back slowly. He glared at her, and she glared right back.

"It was for your own good," she said as soon as he began to move.

"Don't *ever* do that again," he hissed.

"Then don't *make* me do that again," she snarled back. "Now are we going to go, or do I need to use my power to drag you out of here too?"

He withdrew his arm from around her stomach, and

she let his hand go. He mockingly waved in front of her. "After you, sunflower."

She rolled her eyes at him and flicked her hair behind her shoulder, making sure to hit him with it. He made a lighter rumbling sound in his chest, and even though she knew he was upset with her, she smiled. Oddly enough, she found that she liked the feeling of pushing his buttons more than she liked how her normal apologizing attitude made her feel. Johanna filed that away and allowed him to lead them both toward the door and out of the restaurant.

CHAPTER 14

He was pissed. No, he was absolutely fucking *livid*. They were having a wonderful day, and then this fucking asshole had to come and harass *his* mate! Luke wanted to rip into his neck with his bare hands, to watch the fear gather in his eyes right before the life drained out of them. He wanted to bathe in his blood and offer his head to Johanna on a fucking platter.

Logically, he realized that might have been taking it a little too far and that Johanna hadn't asked him for any of those items, but emotionally he didn't give a damn. The moment, the fucking *second* that dipshit had looked at his mate, even had the balls to speak to her, much less in the demeaning manner he had, the best thing he could be was a skinned rug for Johanna to walk over. She deserved so much better, and Luke was tired of hearing—and now having firsthand experience of—her not getting it. If it was that bad when he was there, how bad had it been when he wasn't? No, he didn't need to ask that question. He already knew, and that made everything worse.

He also couldn't believe Johanna had used her powers on him, even if on some core level he knew that she had been right to. Johanna was more important to him than anything, including The Council. He just wanted his mate to be happy and treated fairly. Luke wanted to protect her, and she'd hurt his pride by stopping him from doing as he pleased.

And then she'd had the *audacity* to fucking tease him! He was used to meek and timid Johanna, the side of her that called him to temper himself down, to hold his passions at bay. Did he want to fuck her into oblivion when she was like that? Yes, but that wasn't what she needed from him. She needed his patience, so he gave it to her. She needed him to support her while she worked through everything, to be there for her, and it was easier to remind himself of that when she wasn't tempting the absolute fuck out of him.

She hadn't apologized, and it was clear by the way she was walking in front of him, her back rigid like she was gearing up for a fight either against or for him, that she wasn't going to. It was driving him crazy, as was the way that she walked when she was frustrated, swinging her hips with every step. She was killing him, fucking destroying him, and he was ten seconds away from pulling her behind something and finally sating them both.

It didn't take long for the battle to explode between them. The moment they found a private space on the pier, Johanna rounded on him.

"What the *fuck* were you thinking?" she hissed.

"What was *I* thinking? What were *you* thinking?" he growled back, caging her in.

"*I* was thinking about how much I don't want you to end up dying or whatever type of shit it is that The Council would do to you for harming a human in public. That place was packed, Luke! We wouldn't have been able to make it out of that." She slapped her hands against his chest as if it would put any space between them.

"I don't fucking care about that!" he shouted, refusing to budge from against her.

"Well, I fucking care about you!"

Luke staggered, taking a step away from her. His chest heaved as if she was stealing the very breath from his soul.

"Luke," she said, reaching out to him and gripping onto his shirt. "I don't want to lose you. I will fight whatever and whoever to make sure that doesn't happen, even if it means fighting you."

His heart skipped a beat, and then it pounded so hard under her hand that he was sure she could feel it. He took her in, the way her hair shone and picked up the radiance of the sun's last rays around them, how her blue eyes were so open, so vulnerable to him that he could see the depths of courage and care in them. She was everything, *everything* he could ever want or dream of. She was his *all.*

Luke stepped forward. His arms slid around her waist as he pulled her to him. She made a sound, a ruptured sigh as if he'd stolen the noise from her, then buried her head in his neck. Luke bent forward until he could rest his own head in her neck, listening to the rapid pounding of her pulse under her skin. Her fingers buried into his hair, twisting around the strands. He groaned, his shoulders sagging as his anger left him and fled away into the wind.

"You're killing me, sunflower," he murmured into her skin.

He felt her lips curve against his shoulder, but then her smile fell. Johanna's arms tightened around him as she whispered, "I'd fight and maim and kill everything on this planet before I ever let anything happen to you."

Luke groaned again as fire raged through his veins. He was caught between the swell of pride that his mate would fight for him, the weight of her care, and the knowledge that he would never, *ever* let her put herself in harm's way. His fingers brushed back her hair and he kissed her neck. A soft hum left her mouth as she tilted her head to the side to give him access. He smiled at her trust before traveling upward with soft kisses until he reached her jaw. Then he lifted his head to stare into her eyes while he cupped her cheeks.

"Don't go that far for me, sunflower," he said.

Her eyes burned with conviction as she stared back

at him, but her voice was level and stern when she spoke. "I will if I have to. I'll always do whatever I have to for you, Luke. You're worth it."

He couldn't speak. She was dragging him under. Luke kissed her head and cradled it to his chest. He kept her there, pressed against him, because he couldn't bear the thought of a single shred of space between them. Her fingers twirled strands of his hair, her nails grazing his neck, raising goosebumps over his skin.

Luke closed his eyes and just allowed himself to revel in everything he felt for her: the deep love, the fear and concern that raced through him every time he thought about the dangers she'd been through, the guilt and shame over the moments he hadn't been there to protect her, everything. Telling her was on the tip of his tongue, but he held back, just as he always did, because he didn't want to add more onto her shoulders. He didn't want Johanna to feel as though she owed him anything, or that she needed to rush to meet him somewhere she wasn't ready to be. But this, the quiet times spent in one another's arms? It was in those moments he believed she knew. Even if he didn't say it, she knew everything that was in his heart for her, just like he knew everything that was in hers for him.

The waves lapped at the shore around them. Luke used his hearing to listen to their surroundings and ensure their safety, but he still kept one ear focused on her breathing, her heartbeat, the way her blood flowed through her veins. A little jump started in her heart before she pulled her head back, and he looked down at her. She searched his gaze for something but then her face turned rosy. He grinned. He liked where this was going already.

"Yes, sunflower?"

She licked her lips and his gaze flickered there, capturing the motion before returning to her eyes.

"Back at the bar, you ... you called me your wife."

He smiled and answered unashamed, "I did."

Her breathing hitched in her throat, making his grin grow.

"B-but that means things," she murmured.

"Things?" he said, teasing her. "What things?"

She narrowed her eyes and smacked his arm. "You know what things. Love. Marriage."

"It does? I had no idea."

"Luke!" she said, exasperated, but it only made him laugh harder.

He bent down, his face level with hers, and whispered, "Is there something you're trying to ask me, sunflower?"

She bit her lip and her gaze heated before it slid away from his. He brought it back with a gentle squeeze of her chin.

"I called you my wife because that's how I think of you. You are my mate, the other half of my soul. You delight me, you drive me crazy, and I know now that the reason fate made me immortal was to meet you. I may have called you that word in the heat of the moment, but that's because it's how I feel. My intentions are to marry you one day, my vicious little sunflower, and if you're asking my feelings for you, well…" He smirked. "Yes, I love you."

She gasped, her eyes growing wide at the confession, but it was him who was shocked when her mouth, seconds before in a perfect little "O", pressed against his.

Luke had imagined kissing Johanna more times than he could count. He fantasized about how soft and warm her lips would be, how delicious she would taste, the soft noise she would make when he parted her lips with his tongue. He craved the way she'd sigh into his arms and moan in her pleasure. What he had never imagined, though, was that she would kiss *him* first.

He was so shocked that he hadn't moved, and it wasn't until she pulled back from him, her nervousness visibly morphing into horror, that he sprang into action. Luke cupped the back of her neck and pulled her in for another kiss. His name left her lips in a sigh before their mouths fused together.

There was a moment, just one, where everything felt new. Luke felt as if he was flying, high on the elation coursing through his veins. He'd waited for this single moment for so long, but one kiss wasn't enough. He was greedy, hungry, fucking *starving* for her.

Luke growled low in his throat and Johanna answered with a torn whine that unlocked something in him. His blood heated, raged, and then they turned chaotic. Her hands snaked into his hair, pressing and tugging to keep him close, drawing a groan from him. Luke squeezed her waist, tugging her closer, desperate to eliminate even a tiny breath of air from between them. Then he pushed them back as one, pinning Johanna against the pier. She moaned, the sound going straight to his aching cock.

His fingers slid down her body, reaching her ass. He cupped it and squeezed her flesh, eliciting another moan that set his body aflame. Luke pushed her up, leaning back from the pier to give her just enough room to latch onto him. Johanna wrapped her legs around his back, crossing her ankles behind him. She clung to him, just as mindless and demanding as he was.

He couldn't get enough of her. She tasted like dinner—the slight tang of cheese and seafood, hints of parsley, garlic, and basil mixing with the sweetness of the strawberry daiquiri she'd tried. She was decadent. It was too much, but it was not enough.

Cupping her ass, Luke moved, and when he found the back of a nearby building, he slammed his sunflower against the metal structure. Johanna tugged on his shirt, trying to pull him closer as if she wanted to climb inside his skin.

Luke hid them with his shadow magic, knowing he'd kill anyone who interrupted them. If the world were ending right now, the chaos would have to wait until he was done with her, if he would *ever* be done with her.

He gripped the outside of her thigh, adjusting her

against his body, then he pushed up, tilted his hips, and ground against her core. The sensation was overwhelming even with the barrier of clothes between them, and they both moaned into each other's mouths. Luke did it again and again, showing her all the ways he wished he could be inside her, how he *would* be inside her.

His lips broke away from hers for a torturous second before they found her chin, her jaw, her throat. She tasted divine. He felt her swallow, and the predator in him roared as she tilted her head back against the metal structure and offered him her neck. He almost bit her right then and there, but instead he brushed the back of his hand over her chest, felt the goosebumps that broke out over her skin, and smirked against her collarbone. Then he yanked the tank top and the bra she wore underneath until her breasts popped free. He reveled in how they overflowed from his palms as he licked a path up her neck to her ear.

"Look at you," he purred.

His fingers pulled and squeezed her hard nipples, and she arched her back, pushing more into his hands as she moaned.

"So beautiful, so perfect," he said, his breathing ragged as he devoured her with his gaze. "You would let me do anything I wanted to you."

"Yes," she hissed, tightening her grip on his hair.

"Even out here in the public?" He kissed down to her chest. "Are you into exhibitionism, sunflower?"

"No, I…" She moaned as he kissed her breast softly, slowly. "It's y-you, Luke!"

He looked up at her as his mouth closed around her nipple and he sucked hard. She squeezed his shoulders and wrapped her arms around him as he took more of her breast into his mouth. He bathed her skin with his tongue, marveling at her taste while his fingers trailed lower, down to her jeans. Luke undid their closure. He paused for a moment, breathing in the scent of her desire, and then he slid his fingers under her underwear, running a digit through the slit of her lips.

She gasped, and when he slid two fingers inside of her wet heat, she covered her mouth to muffle her cry.

Luke let go of her nipple and stared into her eyes. They were so dark, so dilated, that they appeared to be jet black, and he was sure they matched his own.

"No one can see you," he said, sliding his fingers out until the tips brushed her entrance. "No one can hear you." He thrust them inside of her again as he ripped her hand away from her lips. "I will *never* let anyone hear you like this. Every sound you make is *mine*. They, just like you, belong to *me*."

She bit her lip and he thrust his fingers harder until she cried out.

"Good girl," he murmured. "That's my good girl."

Luke circled her clit with his thumb, and her whole body shuddered. Her breath caught and she rocked her hips against his hand. He was blown away by the sight.

"That's it, baby, take your pleasure. Show me what you want."

Her hands fisted his shirt as she tried to speak around the moans he tore from her. "I-*Fuck,* I want you, please. I want *you!*"

Luke groaned. "I love the sound of you begging." He brought his lips down to the breast he had yet to taste, making her moan another curse. He licked her nipple and used the opportunity to speak while he continued to thumb her clit. "But you don't need to do that. You have me, sunflower. What more could you want?"

He bit her nipple and Johanna cried out. Her legs tightened around him, thighs flexing as they shook, even as she fought off her orgasm and tried to shove off his leather jacket. When he refused to let her, she huffed, so he curled his fingers, making her cry out once more, "You! I want you! Inside me! Luke, *please!*"

Luke moaned. She was driving him crazy. With a *pop* he released the nipple he was sucking. He could feel his pre-cum leak from his cock as she writhed against him, his fingers pounding in and out of her wet heat. "You want me to fuck you, Johanna? You want me to take you, to fill you with my come?"

"Yes! Yes! Please!" she begged. Her fingers inched lower, and Luke knew he'd be lost if she got anywhere near his dick.

He grabbed both of her wrists with one hand and pinned them above her head The position made her arch her back slightly, and her eyes opened wide at the change, but he didn't give her a moment to adjust. Instead he moved his fingers faster and increased the pressure on her clit until she was shaking.

"Oh, sunflower, I have dreamed nearly every damn day of fucking you. But I'm not going to right now."

"Why?" The word left her mouth as half a plea and half a demand.

Luke curled his fingers again and witnessed her orgasm for the first time. Johanna squeezed her eyes shut as her mouth fell open and she cried out for him. Her legs tightened around his body like he was the only thing keeping her on this planet, while her pussy spasmed around his fingers, gripping them for dear life as if it could somehow take them deeper.

He groaned, his eyes rolling back in his head as he imagined how fucking good it would feel to be inside that hungry little thing, how it would feel to own her, to drown in her wetness and taste every inch of her skin. Luke was famished for her. She was his every wish, every fantasy, every desire, and as Johanna came down from her high, he withdrew his fingers and sucked them clean. He moaned at the taste of her. Saliva pooled in his mouth at the thought of more before she broke him from his train of thought.

"Why?" she asked again, her voice softer, breathless.

Luke ran his fingers up and down the inside of her thighs, wishing he could rip her pants off and enjoy her fully. Her breath hitched as he drew a digit over her flesh, teasing from her pussy up to her clit and back down. She shuddered, and when he slowly slid it inside of her, she let out a hum of pleasure.

"When I fuck you, sunflower, I will take everything from you." He slid his thumb up and down her clit, rubbing the nub as she gasped. "I will take every noise you make, every look you give me, every breath you breathe, every sensation of your skin, every emotion you have, every thought, your blood, even your very soul. I will take *all* that you are in the same way you have consumed *everything* that I am."

He slid two fingers into her, drawing another moan from her lips. "And even after I've taken all of you, I won't stop. I won't stop until we're so tied together that I'm in your veins, Johanna, until you couldn't get me out of you if you tried."

"Luke!" she moaned.

He kissed her until her lips were red, even with his healing magic. He sucked, and nipped, and teased them until they parted, and then he explored her mouth with his tongue, drinking in her taste while he fucked her with his fingers. Luke showed her exactly how he would be with her, and even when Johanna came, he didn't stop rubbing his tongue against hers, nor pressing, rubbing, even pinching her clit, not until she came once more. Only then did this hunger for her begin to calm.

CHAPTER 15

One week. That's how much time had passed since what Johanna now called 'The Incident' at the beach. She still couldn't formulate what happened into proper words. She never expected Luke to tell her that he loved her, nor to let things get so out of hand. His lips, his touch, being pressed up against him the way she had been, had all felt so incredible, but she never would have expected what came after that glorious experience.

Nothing.

Absolutely nothing.

Luke hadn't touched her, at least not in the way she desired to be touched. Sure, he rubbed her back, passed his fingers through her hair, and they still cuddled when they fell asleep, but that was it. Nothing else. He hadn't touched her intimately. He hadn't kissed her either, and it was driving her mad. It felt like they were constantly playing a game where one of them stood in the middle and the other circled them. Round and round they'd go, getting closer and closer until eventually they switched spots, then the cycle would start all over again. They never seemed to be in the same space. Instead, they were constantly teasing, thinking, or working around one another without being on the same page.

It was *infuriating.*

Johanna understood there were several reasons for this. After all, she was still healing from everything. Even she could see how Luke constantly put her care first, so it made her wonder what it was that he saw in her that made him hold back, and how did she make it stop?

She'd tried to figure it out for the first couple of days, to no avail. Then she thought about what he'd demanded if he was going to fuck her. Every time she thought of those words, her blood turned molten, liquid pooled in her belly, and she could barely breathe, much less speak. But she remembered them, every single word, and she'd give it all to Luke, give him everything he wanted … but he wouldn't take it.

No matter what she did or how many times she told him she was his, he didn't seem to believe she meant it. Running out of options, she finally decided to ask Dani for advice. According to her, both of them were incredibly dense, stubborn, and really two peas in the same pod. It was an annoying observation, but one that Johanna did have to agree with—if only slightly.

Johanna had gotten better at voicing what she wanted, at believing she was allowed to want things and to demand nothing less. Yet, until Luke had admitted his feelings for her, she didn't fully believe it could be possible for someone to love her in the way she'd always craved. It made sense that perhaps Luke felt something of that too. Dani even thought that Luke still blamed himself for what had happened to Johanna and couldn't believe her feelings because he didn't think he was worthy of them. That, more than anything else, had spurred her into action, which was the exact reason why Johanna had pushed herself out of her comfort zone and was now lying naked under the covers, waiting for her mate.

An hour had passed by the time Luke's body crossed the threshold into their room. It was a new game he'd started to play with her—waiting until she'd fallen asleep to join her in bed. That was something else Johanna would fix ... later.

She watched as Luke opened a drawer and grabbed a pair of black pants to sleep in.

"What are you still doing up?" he asked as he shut the drawer and turned to face her.

"I was waiting for you."

Luke moved toward her, causing her heartbeat to quicken. Leaning down, he kissed her forehead and then took a deep breath. When his lips parted, she wished they were on her skin again, somewhere lower.

"You didn't have to wait up for me."

"I know, but I wanted to." The beat in her heart fluttered as she admitted, "I missed you."

He sighed, brushing his fingers through her hair at her temple. "I've missed you too. I'll be right there, okay?"

Johanna nodded, turned on her side and watched him disappear into the bathroom. It seemed as if he were gone for an eternity, each second stretching her nerves. When he appeared again, he shut off the light, settling the room into complete darkness. Then he slipped under the covers.

She knew the exact moment he realized she was naked. Luke's breath hitched in his throat, and her heart was beating so fast she thought she might have a stroke.

"You're..."

"Yes," she whispered.

Luke didn't move closer or further away from her. Johanna turned her head to meet his gaze, and even though she couldn't see it in the dark, she could feel it. He was completely focused on her, the intensity of his stare like a tangible force.

When he spoke next, his voice was strained, and a little part of her reveled in it. "Why?"

"Because..." She swallowed hard and tried again. "I want to be your mate, Luke. Make me your mate."

The sheets ruffled behind her, but she didn't move, barely breathed, so scared that something would snap them both out of this moment. Then his chest pressed against her back as he spooned her. She was so relieved that a soft sigh left her lips, but Luke's fingers suddenly slid under her chin, making her tilt her head to meet his eyes. Once her eyes adjusted to the darkness, she saw the fire raging in his.

Luke's mouth moved, but no words came out. His lips parted as he ran his tongue across them and she followed the movement, hyper aware of every little thing he did. Johanna committed to memory every breath he took, the warmth of his body behind her, the feel of the hairs on his arm as they tickled her neck and throat. She wanted it all, because she couldn't stand not having a single piece of him any longer.

Finally he spoke, his voice gravely and low. "Sunflower, are you sure? I need to hear it. I need to know—"

"Yes. *Yes*," she said again, hoping he believed her. Tilting slightly, she cupped his cheek, trying to communicate by touch everything she wished she knew how to say.

He groaned, released a harsh breath, and whispered, "Remember, you asked for this."

Then his lips crushed against hers.

Luke's kisses were all-consuming. He enraptured all her senses and threw her off balance by his gravitational pull, and she loved it. She loved him.

His fingers slid down her throat as he deepened his kiss. Luke moved slowly, deliberately, owning her flesh. His hand cupped her neck, fingers at the sides as he squeezed, choking her. Johanna moaned deep in her throat. Wet heat flooded her core and she squeezed her thighs to ease the ache. She was so sensitive to his touch, so filled with longing that if she wasn't careful, she wouldn't last.

Unconsciously, Johanna rocked her hips back against Luke's, searching for the pleasure only he could provide, and he moaned. He pushed against her, pressing the outline of his erection against her ass as they moaned together. Luke's hand squeezed around her throat again, wringing another moan from her, and she felt like putty in his hands. She was so crazy for him and he hadn't even touched her yet.

Johanna tilted her head back against the pillow, lining her lips with Luke's to deepen the kiss. He groaned as she licked the seam of his lips, and then he opened for her, his tongue pushing into her mouth, licking, flicking, and teasing her own. She buried her hand in his hair to keep his mouth fused with hers. Her other hand was trapped under her body by him, as if he knew how much she ached to touch him.

Luke brushed the back of his fingers from her shoulder down her chest, so slowly it was as if he was completely unaffected in their passionate dance, as if he had all the time in the world. But his rapid breathing and the pounding of his heart against her back told her the truth: he needed this just as much as she did.

Johanna pulled back from him, taking in his face, the soft glow starting in his eyes as she whispered, "Please."

He looked down at her as if he worshipped the ground she walked on, as if her saying the simple word was somehow the most treasured gift she'd ever given him. Then he said, "I've got you, sunflower. I'll give you anything you want."

She shook her head. "Take," she urged, her breath catching in her lungs as he kissed her ear, traced its pathways with his tongue. "Take what you wanted from me."

She felt him smile against her flesh, then his hand grasped her breast, cupping and squeezing it while he ground into her ass. His other hand groped her stomach as he whispered into her ear, "What do you want me to take, sunflower?"

She moaned, arching and pressing into his body, searching more for his touch. "Everything."

"That's so broad, my love." He kissed her neck, and she could feel the sharp points of his teeth press against her skin as the hand on her stomach slid lower. "Tell me what you want me to take," he whispered, trailing a path from her neck to her shoulder. He moaned, as if the simple taste of her gave him pleasure. "Tell me what's mine."

Johanna squeezed the hand that cupped her breast.

"My body," she breathed, and he rewarded her with another squeeze. Then he rolled her nipple with his thumb before pinching the small bud, making her cry out.

"Yes," he moaned. "What else?"

"My heart." It was beating so hard for him, and as his fingers walked along her skin, sliding lower, closer to the place she needed him most, she thought she would lose her mind.

"What else?" he growled, biting her shoulder, grinding harder into her body.

She gasped as his finger finally reached her clit, sliding up and down the bud. "Breath."

"Yes."

She moaned. "Sounds."

"Yes." He circled her clit, tearing another whimper from her lips.

Her head fell back against his shoulder as every nerve ending in her body came alive. "My mind, my soul."

"Yes," he hissed, increasing the pressure on her clit, drawing a tortured cry from her.

"My blood."

He squeezed her breast hard, pinching her nipple, causing her to cry out at the delicious mix of pain and pleasure.

"Good girl," he whispered, rubbing her faster. He was working her closer to an orgasm, an explosion that would send her flying off this planet to the moon in bliss, but she didn't want to go there alone.

Johanna reached behind her with her free hand. She pulled at his pants, pleased that he let her. She was even more pleased when she found his dick free, readily thrusting into her hand. She grasped it, pumped, and he moaned a curse that made her smile.

The speed of his fingers increased and she moaned his name. Johanna spread her thighs. She needed him inside of her *right* now. He grasped the inside of her thigh and moved until his dick was against the lips of her pussy. Then he pushed her thigh down, trapping his cock there, and thrust. Her thighs were soaked in her wetness, making him glide easily. Luke did it again and again. Johanna pushed her hips back, clenching around him and he moaned louder. His fingers pinched her clit, causing her to cry out as more of her wetness pooled between her thighs.

Johanna slid her hand down and rubbed the head of his cock in sync with his thrusts, making him go faster, wilder. Her body jerked against his. She loved the feel of him, loved the thickness between her legs, but she wanted him inside her, and nothing, not even this, not even his fingers on her clit, his lips on her own, or the way he stroked and squeezed her skin would fill that ache. It was a craving. He was the drug, and this was her new addiction, and she wouldn't stop until she got what she wanted, what they *both* wanted.

Luke was close. She could tell in the way he moved,

how he squeezed her hips and pushed her closer to her own orgasm, but she refused to have him come anywhere but inside of her. She *needed* it in a way she couldn't express. The next time his hips jerked back, she grasped his dick, and when he pushed forward, she tilted just enough to get the head of his cock inside of her.

Even though she wanted this, even though she wouldn't go back on this decision, for a split second she wondered what Luke would think of her. But then he was pushing inside of her and every thought, worry, and concern melted from her mind. There was just him, just this.

He pushed, and pushed, and pushed until she curled her fingers in the sheets, holding on for dear life.

"Luke!" she cried.

"I know baby, I know." He groaned, pushing deeper. "You're taking it so well, sunflower."

She moaned his name again, throwing her head back as her pussy throbbed around him.

"There's my good girl. Look at you taking me so deep." He bit her ear and a shudder passed between them. "So good, so perfect," he moaned. "Made for me."

"Yes!"

And then he was seated in her fully. She had never felt so utterly filled and stretched by anything in her whole life. Luke pulled out to the tip before he rammed back inside, making her scream his name. It was one thrust, just one, before she was suddenly in the air.

Then her back was against his chest and she was on top of him.

There was the sound of clothing ripping, and when he spread his legs, now free from the constraints of his pants, he used his knees to spread hers too.

"Luke?" she said breathlessly.

"I wanted to be gentle," he began, "but I can't do that now."

He eased her back down on his cock, spearing her, the position forced her to take him in a whole new way. When he thrust into her to the hilt, she knew she was done for. He gripped her hips and rammed into her, over and over. She shook, spasming against his body, but he kept going. He rested his hand on her stomach and pushed lightly on her belly. A new sensation filled her as she cried out, arching her back, both wanting to escape the pleasure and take more of it at the same time. He wouldn't let her go, she knew that now like she knew the back of her hand. Luke would *never* let her go, never let her get away from him. This was what it meant for him to take her, and she would give everything for him to never stop.

Each thrust was a new shock to her system. Luke rubbed her clit, making her soar to new heights of pleasure. She cried for him, screamed, tears gathering in her eyes, but he kept fucking her in a dirty, thorough claiming of her skin. Her head fell back, and when she linked herself with Luke's thoughts she moaned loudly, knowing he was just as lost as she was.

Then she tilted her head to offer him the last thing she could.

His fangs pierced her skin. The mixture of pain and pleasure as he drank her blood made her release a full body scream that started from her toes and coasted up her body at the speed of a freight train before her cries filled the room and she came. She came so hard she saw stars behind her eyes, and then Luke followed her and she cried out again in joy that finally, *finally* they were one.

———

Luke couldn't help the smile that ghosted his lips as Johanna lay on top of him. Her sweat was mixed with his, her blood flowing through his system. He was still inside of her, and even with all of that, he was still hungry for her. No matter how many times he had her, it would never be enough. But now that he knew he *could* have her, he was willing to try to take his fill.

Her heartbeat was rapidly thumping against his body as he lifted her. He eased out of her slowly, gently, but she was so sensitive she moaned, and the sound went straight to his cock. It twitched for her, already standing at attention to nestle itself back inside her, but Luke had other plans.

He laid Johanna down beside him, and then he rolled on top of her. Her eyes fluttered open to stare up at him. He enjoyed watching the wheels in her head turn as she took in his smirk. He knew the moment the realization hit her because her eyes widened. She cast her gaze down his body, her breath hitching as she saw his erection.

"How?" she asked, and he chuckled at the question as if her pussy hadn't just grown wet at the thought of him inside her again.

"Did you really think once would be enough for me?" He hummed as he nestled between her thighs, making her spread her legs wider for him.

"No," she said, breathless. Then she moaned as his cock slid between her folds. "But so soon?"

"Yes, so soon," he chuckled, the sound cutting into a moan as he slid the tip of his cock between her lips again. "Have you seen yourself? I get an erection every time you walk into a room. It's created a lot of uncomfortable situations."

She laughed, the husky sound traveling over his body.

"And that too," he said, nipping her neck and making her purr.

"My laugh?" Johanna wrapped her arms around his back. She tried to pull him to her, and he chuckled, laving the crook of her neck with his tongue as he settled his weight fully on top of her. The sigh of contentment she gave him made a low growl rumble in his throat.

"Yes. I've wanted you for so long."

Luke pushed up slightly, his fingertips running

through her hair as it fanned around her head. He met her eyes, and another course of satisfaction ran through him as she leveled her gaze at him. She could see in the dark now, better than a normal human. It was a small reminder of what they'd just shared, that she was now immortal, their bond consummated.

"I'm going to spend days inside of your pussy," he whispered gravelly.

"Impossible."

He smiled, accepting her words as a challenge as he kissed down her neck. "Definitely possible and going to happen."

"Luke," she moaned, tilting her head back even as she tried to argue with him. "That is *not* possible." Her breath hitched as he sucked on the base of her throat. "I'll need to eat, and so will you."

"Absolutely," he murmured on her skin as he bit her chest, earning another moan from her. "You'll eat, and I'll eat you. Problem solved."

"Luke—"

"Stop arguing with me."

He cupped her breasts, pinching her hard nipples. Then he ran his tongue between her breasts, along the underside of one mound, and then over her nipple. "It makes me want to ram inside of you and fuck you until the only thing you can do with your mouth is yell my name."

"Oh fuck," she gasped and arched her back.

"Much better."

He sucked one nipple into his mouth, teasing the other with his fingers. He ran his free hand over her stomach, squeezing her flesh and making her moan. A pretty, little blush ran over her skin, but he didn't have to ask why.

"You're beautiful, just like this. Exquisite. I've spent a lot of my life looking at beautiful things, but you? All of them combined could never amount to your beauty." He squeezed and cupped the flesh of her stomach with both of her hands and met her gaze. "This world is stupid."

Luke's fingers reached down to her pussy, no, *his* pussy, and stroked her folds. "One hundred years ago women would have died to look like you. This was healthy." He rubbed over her stomach, then her clit. She bucked, so Luke grabbed her hips and continued his ministrations while holding her gaze. "Your body meant that you could eat well, that you could survive a winter, that you could give birth to healthy children. The rules may have changed, but that doesn't mean a single fucking thing to me, and it shouldn't to you."

He rammed two fingers inside of her and shuddered at her wetness, at the feeling of it tangled with his own come.

"You were beautiful," he said.

He thrust his fingers harder, watched her back arch as she threw her head back and cried out.

"You are beautiful."

He moved faster, curled his fingers, and watched as she started to shake.

"You will always be beautiful."

Then he rubbed her clit, and she yelled his name.

"Say it," he demanded.

She whimpered and he moved faster, pulling another cry from her lips.

"Say it," he repeated. "Say it or I'll stop."

"Yes! Yes!" she cried out.

"Yes, *what*?" he growled, adding a third finger and she damn near came off the bed.

"Luke!"

"Say. It." He commanded, pride and satisfaction pumping through his veins as he watched his mate come undone.

"I'm beautiful," she cried. "I'm beautiful!"

"Good girl," he purred. "Now come on my fingers, I have a meal to enjoy."

Her pussy clenched around his fingers. With three more thrusts, she came, gripping the sheets and crying out in her pleasure. The sound undid him. It unlocked something in his soul that turned him ravenous, and instead of letting her catch her breath, his mouth claimed her core. He kept rubbing her clit in circles, felt the shivers in her spine as she tried to come down from her high, but he wouldn't let her. He pulled his fingers to the tips of her lips, spreading her, and before she could formulate a question he licked between her folds.

She mewed. Her back arched again as he started his

feast, keeping his tongue flat as he slid up and down her pussy lips, tasting them both. She was fucking delicious, like cherries and sugared peaches, and it made him lose all control. He spread her legs further, lifted them over his shoulders and grasped her hips, then he slid his tongue inside of her. She jerked underneath him, and her cries filled the air as he ate her like a starved man.

Luke wasn't satisfied when she came on his lips for the third time in a row, nor when he sucked her clit, slid his fingers back inside of her, and then pierced the flesh of her thigh to drink her blood. Nothing filled him or satisfied his hunger until he knelt between her legs, lined his cock up with her entrance, and thrust home. Only then did he feel complete. Everything before was just the appetizer, but this, here, being inside of his mate where he could take her over and over again was the only thing that sated the beast within him. Here, with his mate's arms around him, her heart beating just as fast as his own, her pussy milking his cock, he felt whole.

Words bubbled out of his throat, things he'd longed to say to her. "Marry me," he moaned against her neck as he thrust harder inside of her.

"Yes!" she shouted without even a moment's hesitation, and it only served to heighten his own pleasure.

He moaned her name. His hands gripped her thighs, spreading and raising them higher as he fit himself deeper inside of her, wishing he could become one with her. "Baby, I'm going to fill you."

Her nails dug into her skin as she moaned, as she fucking begged for it. *"Please!"*

Luke groaned. He didn't stop until he was so deep he was pushing against her cervix. His hand fell to her stomach as he said again, "I'm going to fill you up. I'm going to breed you. I want you pregnant with my child. I want you ... I want *everything* with you."

"Yes!" she moaned, and nodded as if she was trying to make him understand. "Yes, Luke!" She gasped as he hit a new spot in her that had her quivering underneath him, so he did it again. "Luke, yes! Everything. I w-want everything. Oh God! I love you!"

Her confession spurred him. Luke was going so hard, so deep, losing himself so thoroughly in her that he didn't trust himself not to break her. He took her hands and pinned them to the headboard with his own as he kept moving inside her. In time with his thrusts, the headboard slammed against the wall so hard that it creaked. Then the wood splintered and part of the bed broke, tilting them to the side.

He kept going, and the new position drove Johanna fucking wild. Her eyes rolled back in her head, and he was lost, just like her. His fangs broke into the skin of her neck as he drank her blood. It flowed into his mouth, the taste like ambrosia, and when she came around him he swore he'd been blessed. The walls of her pussy tightened around his cock, dragging him under, and he roared out his release. Streams of come shot into her and he kept thrusting, his movements jerky and uneven but enough to draw another orgasm out of his mate. The feeling had him emptying his balls inside of her until he collapsed, broken apart like a shattered vase and put back together with her as the glue.

And just like that, he knew he would never be the same, and he never wanted to be again. Life before her had been a lie. Now there was only Johanna—his sunflower, his stars, his moon, the center of his universe—and the future they would make together, a future that he would spend the rest of his long days cherishing just as much as he cherished her.

CHAPTER 16

Luke hugged Johanna to his side and the smile she gave him blew his heart apart. The venue Dani and Greg had picked for their engagement party was beautiful, as was the love that was so clearly shared between not only the two of them, but everyone in attendance.

But none of it held a candle to his mate.

She looked gorgeous in her black halter top gown that had quickly become his favorite, due to the slit that ran up to her thigh. The opening gave him easy access—which he'd already taken advantage of before they left the house—and based on the way Johanna was looking at him, he'd be taking advantage of it again before they got home.

They approached Dani and Greg and exchanged hugs with them.

"Congratulations, you two!" Johanna said, nodding

to Dani's slightly rounded belly and the diamond glittering on her finger.

Dani looked from her to Luke and smirked. "I'd say congratulations are in store for the two of you too. It's about damn time."

"Dani!" Johanna said with a laugh.

Luke wrapped his arm around her waist and pulled Johanna to his side. "Don't bother, love. She gets a kick out of this."

"Of course I do, especially when I'm right," Dani said and they all shared a laugh.

Luke bent down to Dani's stomach and gently patted her belly. "How's my niece or nephew?"

"Keeping the both of us up all night," Dani said, curling into Greg's side.

"Already?" Johanna asked.

"Well, our little one is already telling me what they prefer to eat, and if I try anything else I have a horrible case of nausea."

Luke frowned. "Is our healing magic not working?"

Greg shook his head. "I think it's because Ella's human, and since we're still in the first trimester it's too early to change her into a vampire."

Luke coughed into his hand to keep from laughing at the look Dani gave Greg when he said 'we,' as if he was also carrying the baby. But then it cleared, and Dani smoothed Greg's furrowed brows. "You worry too much."

They shared a look which Johanna caught. "Is everything okay?" she asked.

Dani and Greg shared another look and then they both stared at Luke. He understood immediately: Zachariah.

Johanna shifted by his side, drawing his gaze. "Go ahead and talk, I'll just—"

"No," Luke said.

"Stay, really," said Dani.

"We just don't want to make you uncomfortable," Greg added.

Johanna lips turned upward, but the action didn't match her blank eyes.

"I want you to stay, but only if talking about this won't hurt you," Luke said to her telepathically as he squeezed her hip.

She nodded to him. "I'll be fine. Please, go ahead."

Dani sighed. "We still haven't found him."

Greg ran his fingers through her hair. "And he's been entirely too quiet for my liking."

"How many of the coordinates have you been able to visit?" Johanna asked.

"Almost all of them. At first, we'd at least find some of his people," Dani said.

"But lately the locations have either been vacant or full of traps." Greg's tone softened as he addressed Johanna. "I think he knows that you're with us, and we're concerned he's just biding his time. Ella and I actually discussed canceling this event."

"I'm happy you didn't. You both deserve this. He shouldn't get to ruin it," Johanna said, her voice so stern that Luke knew she wasn't just talking about what Greg and Dani deserved, but what she deserved as well.

"Johanna's right," Luke said. "This is a celebratory event, and an important one. We all need tonight." He patted Greg's shoulder. "I'm happy you didn't cancel."

Greg nodded, yet the frown on his face didn't disappear.

"I..." Johanna began, then she rolled her shoulders back and met their eyes. "I'm sorry I still can't remember anything. I can't be of more help in that regard, but I can at least help you to ease your mind now if you're concerned about security."

Greg's eyebrows rose. "Really? How?"

"A psychic net. I can connect to each person's mind here and create a net. If someone sees any type of suspicious activity, it's immediately reported back to all of us at the same time. That way we can make sure Dani and the baby are safe while also investigating the issue," Johanna explained.

Luke rubbed her hip. "Doesn't that use a lot of magic?"

Johanna shook her head. "No, it's rudimentary for me. It's more of a dormant thing that will only be activated when the criteria is met."

Dani squeezed her hand. "That would be amazing. Thank you, Jo."

Johanna looked pleased with herself, but Luke still

wasn't sure. He leaned down and dropped a kiss on her temple while he spoke to her again telepathically.

"If you push it, sunflower, I will take you into the nearest room and spank that gorgeous ass of yours. This is your only warning."

She blushed before replying, *"That isn't much of a warning when you were already planning on getting me alone."*

He smirked into her hair. *"Keep being a cheeky brat and I'll make sure everyone at this party hears you scream when I fuck you."*

Her blush darkened. *"Shut up! I can't concentrate when you do that."*

Luke chuckled but did as she said. He held her closer while he felt the pressure of her magic. It flitted, dancing around them like a ballerina for several seconds. Then the pressure eased to something of a tingle at the back of his mind, and he knew that was her net.

A few moments later Johanna's face lit up in delight. "There, it's done. It isn't much, but hopefully it will be enough to help the two of you have a good time tonight."

Dani and Johanna shared a hug. "Thank you so much."

"Of course!" Johanna smiled.

Luke wrapped his arm around her shoulder. "Now if you excuse us, I need to have a word with my mate."

Johanna's eyes widened and she blushed again,

making Dani and Greg laugh before Luke led her away and made good on his promise.

———

"Luke!" Johanna yelled, laughing as he closed the door to their house behind them. "Put me down!"

He smacked her ass, making her yelp. He did it again, then squeezed and caressed her flesh. The sting coupled with his touch made her moan. She tried to shift off his shoulder once more, but he held her steady.

"What was it you were saying, sunflower?" Luke stepped into the kitchen, "Ah, that's right. Something about putting you down." He jumped, making her stomach free fall as she screamed from the movement, then he set her onto the counter.

"Luke!" She laughed, bracing his shoulders. "Would you stop tossing me around like a rag doll?"

"It's about time you get used to it, sunflower. Now open up and feed me that pussy, baby." He tapped her knees. "I'm hungry."

A shudder ran through her. There was nothing she could do but obey him when he spoke to her like that. She spread her legs wide to accommodate him. Luke cupped the back of her knees and pulled her to the edge of the counter as he pressed his body against hers.

They attacked each other in an instant. His mouth descended on hers and she pulled at him, wrapping her legs around his waist, keeping him where she wanted him. A low rumble left his throat as he pressed his hips into hers and ground against her already wet core.

Johanna moaned into his mouth and shoved his jacket off him, elated that she was one step closer to having his flesh against hers, but frantic and needy to have more.

Luke broke the kiss. He licked and nipped down her neck, sucking on her skin as his hands roamed up her back. "I like this dress on you," he said in a gravely whisper, "but if you don't tell me how to get it off, I'll rip it to shreds."

"Neanderthal," she gasped.

Luke aligned his erection, pressing hard against her core as he rocked their hips. "Five seconds," he warned.

"It's on the side!"

Luke hiked her dress up and she lifted her hips, jerking against him as her bare bottom hit the cold counter.

"Good girl," he growled, and her thighs clenched around him.

Luke found the closure and opened it, helping Johanna to pull the material over her head. He paused as she sat nearly naked on the counter, the same glorious, adoring gaze filling his eyes. He took her in, looking over every bit of her skin as if he were memorizing her body. "I will never get enough of you."

Then he was on her.

Her bra was tossed away and his lips replaced the fabric, licking, sucking, and biting her flesh. She arched into his embrace. Her hands slid down his chest, pulling up at his tucked shirt until it was free. Then she reached for his belt and unbuckled it. Undoing the button underneath, she carefully unzipped his pants around his engorged cock.

He hissed, then yanked her hands away and pinned them behind her. She moaned, jerking and struggling to get free.

Luke raked his teeth over her nipple, causing her to gasp and her toes to curl in her heels. "I need to taste you first."

She pushed her hips against his. "Luke, I need you."

He smiled and stood, reaching his full height. "And you'll have me. But this hungry little thing right here?" He slid his fingers down to her pussy, cupping her lips before he spread them and teased her entrance, drawing a moan from her. "She'll take anything I offer her, won't she?"

She moaned his name and her head fell back.

"Won't she?" He bit her lip, drawing it into his mouth.

"Y-Yes! Yes!"

Luke kissed her but refused to let go of her wrists. Instead, he delved deeper inside of her, his fingers strumming her like a guitar, guiding her like the conductor of an orchestra. He knew all the chords, all the ways to make her reach new highs she didn't know she could. He pursued her, corned her, trapped her, until all she could see, feel, taste, smell, even think of was him. And she let him, and she would let him for the rest of fucking eternity.

She came with his fingers thrusting into her, his taste on her lips, trapped against his body. She came so fucking hard, and then he angled her in a way that she had no choice but to lay back while he made her come over and over again. He licked, sucked, bit, nipped, touched, rubbed, thrust, and fucked her with his fingers so many times she lost count, and she took it all. Johanna kept her legs over his shoulders, tangled her fingers in his hair. She rode him every time he entered her, her hips jerking and moving of their own accord until she reached her completion.

Luke was right; she was hungry for him, and it was a hunger that would never be filled.

Finally he lifted his mouth from her, and her legs fell away. A small smile graced her lips as she knew that soon they would be joined. Johanna was frantic for it, for his cock, for the feeling of having him so deep inside of her that it felt like he was part of her.

He pushed his pants and boxer briefs down, and she sat up to take his length in her hands. Luke groaned, his head falling back as she pumped up and down his shaft. He was hot, like magma in her palms. Johanna was so far gone that when a bead of pre-cum appeared at the tip, she swiped it with her finger and sucked the taste of him into her mouth.

Luke lost control. In one fell swoop he entered her, but it wasn't enough for either of them. His hands found her ass as he pushed and she pulled, wanting the entirety of her body plastered against his. He knew, understood without her even saying a word or sending the thought to him, and in another second she was pressed against the cold refrigerator. The temperature difference sent chills up her body, but she was too crazed by Luke to notice.

His scent was all over her, something warm and spicy, a mixture of mint, oranges, and vanilla. It made the flames between them burn even higher, and every single one of his thrusts had her crying out his name. But still she wanted more, and more, and more. She wanted him inside her in a way no one else could ever be. She wanted to be full of him, constantly, *always*.

"Luke!" she moaned, her heels digging into his ass, her nails pushing into his back.

"I know baby," he moaned. "I know. I feel it too."

She groaned and her eyes fell to his neck. He swallowed and she wanted to taste … to drink.

"Wait!" Johanna said and Luke immediately froze.

Even in his breathless voice, his concern was evident. "Are you okay? Did I hurt you?"

"No." She cleared her throat, trying to regain her voice, her breath. "No, but I … I want…"

She licked her lips. She didn't know where this was coming from. Maybe it was connecting with so many vampires earlier, or the pleasure she felt when Luke drank from her, or maybe it was her desire to be stronger, to protect him. Maybe it was everything, but she needed this so much that she would get on her hands and knees and beg if that's what it took to get his blood inside of her.

"I want to drink your blood."

He shook his head. "What did you say?"

"I want to drink your blood."

Luke swallowed, and even though she didn't feel his hips move, she swore that somehow he grew inside of her. Her pussy tightened around him in response and they both moaned.

"Sunflower," Luke groaned. "You can't do that."

"Please. Please, I-I need it."

Luke cupped her face. "Baby, if you drink my blood like that, you'll become a vampire."

She met his darkened eyes. "I know."

He groaned her name, squeezing his eyes shut as if she were torturing him.

"I know I'll become a vampire. I want to be one."

His arm came to rest on the fridge, followed by his head as he mumbled incoherently.

"Please," she said again.

Luke was quiet for a moment before he whispered. "Why?"

"Because I want to be as strong as you. I want to be able to protect you, and I-I *need* it." She rocked her hips, drawing a moan from both of them.

His lips latched onto her ear as he slowly rolled his hips, thrusting inside of her. "Tell me why you need it, sunflower."

"Because I *crave* you!" She hissed as he bit her ear, the words tumbling out of her. "I need to be full of you, I need to always have you in me. I need you, *please!*"

"Oh fuck," he said moaned as he held her hips and rammed inside of her hard.

She let out a cry, but frustration built in her when he didn't do it again.

"Grab the knife to your right," he said, his lips brushing her skin with every word.

Even in her shock she found herself listening, reaching for the blade, excitement coursing through her veins.

"You'll have to cut me here," he said, tracing the artery of his neck.

"Will it hurt you?"

"No, I'll be fine. But you have to understand that this will change you. You'll be faster, stronger, *hungrier* for years until you learn how to control yourself."

"I understand. Can I now, please?" Johanna asked, scared that he'd change his mind if she asked any more questions.

"Yes, whenever you'd like—Ah!"

And then she was sucking at his skin, drinking his blood. The first gulp was acidic, fatty, but as she gulped down more she began to notice something else, flavors that she shouldn't be able to taste. Then Luke started ramming into her uncontrollably and she couldn't stop. She held him, grasping him to her as close as possible while he made her mindless in her pleasure against the refrigerator.

Johanna lifted her head and cried out as he claimed the very essence of who she was. Her veins felt as though they'd expanded, shooting fire and lightning through her body. She wanted more. Her lips found Luke's neck again and her teeth, now pointed, dug into his skin, ready to feast. She didn't have time for shock or confusion, she was too desperate, too *crazed* for him.

He cried out, bucking inside of her like a wild beast, and she took him and drank from him, her moans muffled against his skin. Luke buckled, sliding down to the floor, then his hand weaved into her hair and he pulled her back. His lips found her neck, teeth sliding in as he fed on her blood. She screamed, writhing, jerking, pushing, and pulling against him as her orgasm coasted through her veins.

And then she *felt* his, felt each trail of come as it shot inside of her, felt the way her pussy spasmed around him in both her pleasure and his. Testing the new sensation, she scratched her nails down his back and felt as if he'd done the same thing to her. Immediately, Luke was hard, and just as quickly he pounded into her, pushing her into the floor with his body. Their linked pleasure was too much, and they came together soon after, and again, and again, and again, losing track of time, their surroundings, everything except one another.

CHAPTER 17

Luke ran his fingers though her hair and they both let out a soft sigh.

Johanna snuggled more into his chest, her fingertips gently stroking his shoulder. "Remind me why you have to go again," she murmured, tickling his skin with her lips.

He chuckled. "Because, my dear, sweet sunflower, you're a vampire now, and The Council likes to keep track of newly turned vampires."

She hummed. "That sounds like something that could be easily taken care of with a phone call."

Luke let out a bark of laughter and held her closer to him. "Is this your way of saying you'll miss me?"

Johanna's lips curved into a smile against his neck before she lifted her head and kissed him sweetly. "No, that's my way of saying I'll miss you." She ran her fingers through his hair, tousling it. "Why do you have to go, really?"

"Greg already petitioned for our mate bond with The Council. By going, I'll be reinforcing that by letting them know that you've been turned, while also taking care of a couple of other things."

She hummed again. "Why did he have to petition for us?"

Luke sighed. "The Council cannot interfere with a mate bond pair, if that's what you're asking. But if a vampire loses their mate, it can be catastrophic for the rest of our species. It's the same for the other immortals. There have been cases of immortals going on killing sprees, abusing their powers, turning people against their will. The loss utterly destroys them, and at that stage they have nothing to lose.

"When Greg goes to petition for a mate bond or mated couple, he agrees to be held responsible for any incidents their mate bond may cause. If one of the mated pair is in danger, Greg will help to get them out. If one of the mated pair dies, Greg will be there to assist and take care of the surviving mate. But if one of the mated pair decided tomorrow to wage war on the world, Greg will be the person who cleans up the mess, and also who The Council will blame."

Johanna gasped. "That's horrible! That shouldn't be completely on him."

Luke nodded. "I agree with you, but unfortunately that's the pressure they put on him. When I go to The

Council today, I will re-petition them to share the responsibility of our mate bond and of anything that happens now that you're a vampire."

He kissed her head. "I trust you. You're doing well with your cravings, strength, and speed, but it's just something that must be done. It will also be a way to prove to them that I am taking more responsibility with our circle, like we talked about, and help Greg to not worry as much while Dani is pregnant."

Johanna's hand slid from his shoulder up to the back of his neck as she massaged his skin. "It'll be good for him. And for you too, I think."

He kissed her head. "Yeah, it will be."

———

Luke had a huge smile on his face as he drove back to their house. The meeting had gone well. He had believed it would, but as this was his first time implementing himself in The Council's dealings, he had been nervous.

But much like Johanna had suspected, that wasn't the real reason he'd gone. Luke needed to access The Council's archives. According to Johanna, her family had participated in past vampire wars and killed their fair share of them. The Council had files on every war and the participants, whether they won or lost, and Luke wanted to use that to find Johanna's family.

Something in his blood sang when he opened their

folder. If that wasn't enough, Johanna had told him she looked the most like her grandmother, and she was right. They had been nearly identical in their twenties.

He only hoped that when he showed his sunflower, it would make her happy. She hadn't spoken about her family in quite some time, but every so often he'd catch a sad expression on her face, as if she were missing something or someone. While Johanna hadn't said anything negative about her family and it was clear she loved them very much, he didn't know them and wasn't sure if he was doing the right thing. Still, Luke reasoned it was only right to at least try. After all, Luke planned to ask them for their blessing to marry Johanna, and he couldn't do that if he never found them.

But as Luke pulled up to his and Johanna's house, his joy faded away. Something was wrong. There was a heavy weight in the air, so stifling that as he exited the garage, he crumpled to the floor.

He realized immediately that it was Johanna. This was the same pressure she had used when she held him down in the cave, only now it was ten times worse, wide and crushing. Luke didn't understand what had happened, but he knew he had to get to her. He had to keep her safe.

He couldn't walk or even crawl to find her, so he dematerialized into shadow. Even then he could still feel her power. He searched for the shadow of other items and used them to propel himself forward and throughout the house until he found her floating above the couch, dangling by her waist as if held by an invisible string.

His senses told him no one had entered the house, nor was there anyone in the surrounding area. So what had triggered her to use her power like this?

Luke blended into Johanna's shadow. He reached for her but was only met with pain. His arm felt as if it had been crushed under a steamroller, but he didn't care or acknowledge the agony he felt. He would heal, but his mate was in danger and nothing would be right in the world again until she was safe.

"Johanna!" he screamed out to her.

The unbearable weight that held him down dissipated, pulled back into Johanna so fast that it created a vacuum effect, knocking objects and tossing pieces of furniture as if they were nothing. Her power hit her like an internal combustion, and she began to fall through the air.

Luke materialized and caught her, cradling her in his arms as he settled her on the couch.

"Johanna?" he called, but she still didn't open her eyes. "Come on, sunflower, don't do this to me again."

Still, no response.

"Baby, *please*," he begged, cupping her cheek. "Please, I need you."

Her eyelids fluttered and she looked up at him, but it wasn't the stare he was used to. She looked at him like it was the first time she was seeing him, truly seeing him, and he realized then what was different. In her eyes he saw pain, agony, and heartbreak. Darkness roamed there freely, only clearing when a small ray of hope rushed to the surface as she finally focused on him.

"Luke?"

"Baby, I'm right here. I'm *right* here," he said, trying to convince them both that everything was alright, that there was no reason for the sudden, frantic beating of his heart.

Then her eyes watered, and she sobbed. Her arms wrapped around his neck so tight that she would have choked him if he were human. She cried his name over and over, the only word among her screams and heartbreaking wails.

Luke held her to his chest, his heart breaking just as much as hers seemed to be, because it suddenly all made sense. This wasn't because he'd been gone for a few hours. She clung to him as if he'd been gone for days, for months, and there was only one realization that he could come to from her reaction.

She finally remembered everything.

———

The next few days were difficult for them. Johanna had regained her memories, and they had wrecked her. The first day she had allowed him to hold her while she cried. She barely ate unless he forced a cup of blood into her hands, and she wouldn't sleep unless he held her so close that she could barely breathe. Only then did she seem to feel any sort of peace.

The next day she was trying to conquer the world. She asked him to call his family so she could relay the information she had about Zachariah and his inner workings. Johanna never once brought up what happened to her while she had been held captive, but he knew she remembered. She'd closed her mind to him. He felt robbed of their connection, but Luke knew it wasn't for her benefit. It was for his. It was obvious in how she recounted her story, in the pauses, deep breaths, the small shudders and flinches she unconsciously made even while he stood behind her and held her.

His presence didn't seem to be enough to take away the pain she felt. Luke knew it was irrational to hope it would be, but it stung nonetheless. The only thing that counteracted his shattered pride was watching Johanna's perseverance, and he hated that as much as he was honored by it. Even while she was hurting, even while she seemed to be dying inside, she put all of that aside. Her sole purpose was to help them win this war and save as many tortured immortals as she could.

Her information was invaluable. Johanna explained that Zachariah was a pseudo-leader, nothing more than a puppet. The real leader was a woman who went by the name of Constance. Johanna didn't believe she was a vampire, although she did seem to have some vampiric abilities. Instead, her real talent was the magic to possess someone. That was the magic Johanna had been under for six months.

Johanna was kidnapped by Zachariah after visiting her grandmother in the hospital. He moved her to another location and forced her to drink a bowl of Constance's blood, which contained trace levels of magic. After that, she was no longer herself. Everything she said and did was under Constance's command. Constance and Zachariah planned to use her to gain information on Greg and the inner workings of The Novak Firm and their circle.

Because Johanna's abilities dealt with the mind, she was able to block part of herself away. Whenever Constance or Zachariah asked her to report back to them, Johanna told them she wasn't high enough in the company to learn anything. During that time she had tried to get help, and for that they killed her grandmother. They would have killed her too, but in her rage Johanna came out of her possession and used her abilities on Zachariah. That was how he found out she could control another's mind, and after he and his allies subdued her, he began to feed on her and use her as his aid.

She also told them that she knew Erik. In fact, he had been her friend and had helped to keep her sane while she was stuck in that hellhole. Then she delivered the final blow: If they had gone fifty feet further down the same passage in the caves where they'd found the women, they would have found him too.

That broke Mya, but Johanna quickly assured them that he was still alive. Erik was the reason Constance and Zachariah had enhanced healing abilities. Constance needed him as she routinely siphoned his blood to try to enhance the strength of the rest of the vampires that served her. As far as Johanna knew, her attempts had failed, but Constance could have succeeded in the time Johanna had been with Luke.

The information Johanna had given was beyond beneficial but had also left everyone drained. Everyone but her. The moment Dani, Greg, and Mya left, Johanna set to work. She grabbed the paperwork containing her coordinates and tore them apart. Luke tried to get her to rest, but she explained that she knew of a few more locations and she wanted to make sure she noted them down. She believed that while Zachariah may have abandoned some of the places they'd raided, these were his acting home bases and he wouldn't leave them willingly.

Luke sighed and agreed with her, but he'd noticed a pattern. Every time he came to check on her, she did a double take when she saw him, as if she expected someone else. If he stood in the doorway and called her name, she almost jumped out of her skin. Each time she told him she was fine, and each time he suggested she rest and come back to her work tomorrow, she shook her head and ignored him.

Finally, Luke had had enough. He approached her,

saying her name as softly as he could, but it had the same effect. He couldn't take it anymore.

"Sunflower, you've done enough now. Why don't you—"

"No," she said, not looking up from the papers strewn around her. "I'm not done yet."

"Baby, you've been at this for hours."

"It's fine. I'm fine. Just let me finish."

"Johanna—"

She whirled around to face him. "No!"

Luke took a step toward her, his arms held out to take her in his embrace, but she flinched.

He froze entirely. Slowly her face changed from one of fear to horror. His throat felt like sandpaper as the realization fell from his lips. "Are you scared of me? Do you see *him* when you look at me?"

"No!"

Luke took a step back.

"No! No, *please*," Johanna said again. She reached for him, her fingers grasping onto his shirt. The warmth of her body seeped into his, but he didn't know how to react, how to move, or if moving at all would frighten her more.

"Luke, I swear I don't see him. I don't see him when I look at you."

She was manic now, shaking her head, and when he finally closed his arms around her, he felt the visceral shudder through her system. Then she began to tremble.

"I'm not scared of you," she said, her eyes swimming in tears. "I'm scared *for* you."

"Sunflower," he began, but the single tear that rolled down her cheek made him pause. Hesitantly, he cupped her face, and she choked back a sob as he wiped the tear away.

"He threatened you every day," she whispered. "Every single day. Every time I thought about running away, every time I thought about trying to get help. I even..." She paused, biting her lip hard, as if that pain was better than the one pouring out of her and into him. "I threatened to kill myself if he went after you."

Luke gasped. He could never imagine a world without her in it, and that she was willing to kill herself for *him* ... He shook his head, speechless.

"He told me that if I did that, he'd kill you. I don't doubt you, Luke. I swear I don't. But..." She looked away from him for a moment so he rubbed her cheeks, bringing her gaze back to his. "I know what he did to me. I know everything he did to me. I don't want, no, I can't *stand* the idea of him ever doing that to you. I need to find him."

Johanna reached back, extracting herself from his arms to gather the papers in her hands. She shook as she held them, presenting them to him as if they were the secret key she had spent her life searching for. "If I can find him, if I can kill him, he can't hurt you. I just need to figure this out."

She slammed the papers back on the table and

stormed back to him. He met her halfway, pulling her into his arms with an angry sigh.

"I can do this," Johanna said as she rested her head over his chest. "I have to do this for you, for Mya and Erik, for whoever else he's holding captive right now. I can do this. I *have* to do this."

Luke held her as he tried to steady the rage building within him. Johanna didn't need his rage. She needed his empathy, and he would give her all that he was.

"Do you love me?" he asked her.

She clutched onto his back, pressing her body into his as if she could swallow him whole, as if she could merge their bodies in some way. "More than life itself."

"And I love you just as much. Tell me, sunflower, if I was the one going through all of this, what would you say to me? What would you want me to do?"

Her head snapped up as her wide eyes met his, and he knew he had her. Johanna struggled doing things for herself, Luke knew that, but he realized that if he made himself the example then her love, her need to protect him, would outweigh anything else and she wouldn't be able to argue. Instead, she would be forced to see reason.

Johanna tilted her head down and away from his, but he gently grasped her chin and made her meet his eyes. "Tell me."

"I'd..."

"You'd make me rest. You'd take care of me, support me, do anything and give me anything I needed to renew my strength." Luke ran his fingers over her skin. "You'd wipe away all my fears and fight all of my battles with a smile on your face, wouldn't you, my sweet sunflower?"

"Y-Yes," she hiccuped, fighting back tears.

"Then let me do this for you. You are my love, my everything. What hurts you, hurts me. What frightens you, frightens me. If there is something you want to fight or kill, *I* will be your weapon and your shield. Let me fight with you, please. Aren't we better together?"

She nodded, more tears falling down her face that he kissed away. "But I-I don't know how."

"First, come rest with me. Then we'll attack your internal battles full on, whether you want to fight them together, or if you'd be willing to consider getting an outside perspective, such as therapy. I'll even go with you."

"B-But the coordinates—"

He shushed her softly, tucking her hair behind her ears. "They'll still be there. You've gone through so much, sunflower. It's time to rest. It's okay to rest. We'll look at them tomorrow."

Johanna bit her lip, clearly battling a war inside herself.

Luke slowly let his hands slide down her neck, over her shoulders, and down her arms until he reached her hands. He squeezed her hands in his and held them as he brought them to his lips and kissed them both.

"Come with me, sunflower. I don't want to sleep without you."

She bit her lip again but nodded.

Hope flared to life inside of Luke, and as they left the room together, he knew they would get through this. It may be a long, turbulent road, but they would see the other side, and he felt grateful to have someone who would fight just as hard for him as he would for her.

CHAPTER 18

Agreeing to therapy was a difficult thing for Johanna. It hurt her pride to have something wrong with her. It hurt to have to reach out to someone else. She was a mental witch, having trained her mind for years to be able to deal with her powers, to go inside other's heads and come out unscathed. And yet, here she was.

Her appointment with Estelle had lasted an additional hour over what they'd scheduled. Estelle had worked with several of the women Greg, Dani, Luke, and Mya had saved from the caves, which is why she believed she would also be able to help Johanna.

At first, Johanna was nervous. Estelle began with rudimentary questions which Johanna answered honestly. Then Estelle simply said, "Have you always felt like you needed to be the hero?"

"The hero?" Johanna asked.

"Yes, that the only time you have worth and value is

when you're rescuing someone else from their perils. That if you've sacrificed yourself for the greater good, then it was all worth it because you've served your purpose."

Johanna's mouth fell open. She didn't even know she was crying until she felt the wetness roll down her cheeks. In just a few moments, Estelle had ripped into Johanna's psyche and unveiled a truth so close to her heart she thought she could hide it forever. The façade fell apart, just as Johanna did at the seams, and she cried. She cried as she told her story to Estelle, she cried as she talked about her childhood, she cried as she talked about the abuse she'd gone through and how robbed she felt of everything—another truth she kept to herself for fear that it was selfish.

Estelle listened and handed her tissues while Johanna opened her entire heart. She never rushed her, never quieted her, didn't even take notes. She just listened, and Johanna didn't realize how much she'd needed that.

When she finished, Estelle told her that she believed Johanna had PTSD. She explained there were different types of PTSD, and that war had many different faces. Because she wanted to know, Estelle walked Johanna through what she thought was the best course of action. First, journaling. Johanna needed to get in touch with her emotions and make time for them instead of blocking them off to try to function throughout her day. Between that, talk therapy, and mindfulness practices, she believed Johanna would be just fine.

Luke took her to get an actual notebook, as she figured she'd procrastinate journaling if she used something electronic, and the next day she tried it. She sat in the sunroom, pulled out her notebook, opened to the first page, and wrote: *This is stupid.*

The dismissive words shocked her. She froze with her pen in her hand, her heart beating a mile a minute as if she were not allowed to voice her innermost feelings and thoughts this way. Then she took a deep breath and reminded herself that she was. She had to do this to get better, and she could judge herself for what she wrote later. Now she could just be free.

This feels like a waste of time. I feel like I should be doing twenty million other things. We still haven't found Zachariah; I'm still having a hard time correcting the last few coordinates and remembering exactly when I switched from one coding system to another because it all just takes me back. I remember how everything felt, how hopeless I felt. I truly believed there would be no way out. I truly believed I was going to die.

Her hand shook at the revelation, but she couldn't stop now.

I wanted to die. I didn't want to feel guilty anymore. I didn't want to be hurt anymore. Death would have been so much easier.

Johanna broke down, crumbling over the table. Luke was at her side in an instant and she turned into his embrace. He picked her up and carried her, sitting with her on one of the couches while she cried into his shirt. He rubbed her hair and stroked her back, but otherwise said nothing. He never asked what happened to make her cry, or what she'd written. He was just there throughout it all.

———

By her next session, Johanna was excited to start meditation, to do *anything* else but fucking cry. She had never cried so much in her entire life, and she was tired of it. Estelle, on the other hand, thought she was making progress, but Johanna couldn't see it herself.

Estelle says I need to cut myself some slack. It's not that I don't believe her, I just don't know how to. That's the problem, isn't it?

Johanna sighed.

I feel as though I have more problems than solutions, and sometimes it doesn't seem worth it at all. I feel weak. I feel pitiful. I feel like the world is just moving around me while I'm stuck standing still. Every time I try to move with it, I fall into a pothole, or a sewage drain, or something. But even all of that feels ridiculous.

I'm here. I'm alive right now. I'm living and breathing and safe. I'm safe, and yet I've never felt more afraid. I remember feeling like this when I regained consciousness, that if I reached out too far, if I hoped just a little too much, that everything would come crumbling down and it would all be my fault. It would serve me right for trying.

But I want to try. I wish I didn't, but I want to.

Johanna sat up straighter in her chair as her resolve burst through her.

Dani's wedding is in less than three months, and by then I will be better. That's a promise to me and to everyone I love.

I won't give up.

———

As excited as Johanna had been for her meditation practices, it wasn't going well. She couldn't seem to sit in the quiet and train her mind to turn off. Each time she closed her eyes, another thought, another feeling, another longing emerged and buzzed around her head until with a frustrated sigh she opened her eyes.

The moment she did, Luke appeared in the doorway with what looked like a yoga mat.

"What are you doing?"

"You've been having a hard time with meditation, so I thought I'd come try it with you."

A small smile graced her face as he lined the mat up in front of her own. "You don't have to do that."

"I know, but I want to," he said, sitting down to face her.

Johanna tilted her head to the side as he settled in. "I know you want to help, and I appreciate it more than

I can ever tell you, but having you in front of me is only going to distract me more."

He smirked, and she realized just how much she'd missed that little knowing curl of his lips.

"Glad to see you're still interested, but no. This is couples' meditation. I found a guided meditation app and figured that might help you since it will be something to listen to. Afterward we can do the couples' breathwork session, if you'd like to give it a try," he said softly.

Johanna reached out and squeezed his hand. "Yes, I would. Thank you for doing all of this for me."

Luke cupped her cheek. She closed her eyes, feeling the warmth of his palm on her skin.

"I will always do anything I can for you. Remember, we're in this together."

He started the app and Johanna followed its instructions. It guided her to breathe in and take in the scents around her, so she focused on Luke's unique fragrance. It filled her nostrils just as his heartbeat and breathing filled her ears, and she sighed. The tension in her body settled down as Johanna fell into a rhythm with him, and then the guided meditation ended and she wondered where the time had gone.

Luke opened his eyes and seemed to be just as lost as she was. He held out his hand to her and she took it. Then he spread his legs, picked her up, and deposited her on his lap. She squeaked and he laughed.

Johanna wrapped her legs around him. He pulled

her close and they just held one another. She could feel the beating of his heart, so strong it felt like it was her own. She felt the rumble of his chest as each breath filled and left his lungs. The tickle of his body hair awakened her every nerve ending, and yet she'd never felt so peaceful in her entire life.

They stayed like that for minutes, maybe even hours. All she knew was that in that moment she felt as though they were one, and it was the most beautiful thing she'd ever experienced.

After a while, Luke slipped his arms from her back and she did the same, believing he meant to pull away entirely, instead he took her hand and laid it over his heart. Then he did the same with his hand over hers. He rested his forehead against her own, and they shared their breaths.

Then he whispered to her, "Together."

She whispered the word back, meaning it with every ounce of her heart, and a little more of her anguish slipped away.

———

She was pissed.

Johanna had finished putting together all the coordinates and was overjoyed at the prospect of Zachariah finally being dealt with, but he wasn't at any of the locations. Johanna checked her work again and again, thinking maybe she'd messed up a set of numbers and had thrown everything else off, but that wasn't the case. He truly had up and abandoned every place she knew of, which confirmed several things for her.

Zachariah knew where she was. He knew who she was with and what she had done, but the most terrifying of all the conclusions was that his army was growing. If he had retreated, it meant that he was either kidnapping more people or turning more vampires against their will.

She knew how it happened. The trauma broke their minds and Zachariah used that to imprint on them the same way a mother did to her ducklings. He offered them food and a home if they did his bidding, and they almost always agreed. She'd seen it more than enough times to count, and it wasn't fucking fair!

And this anger, this fucking wrath, settled into her bones. She couldn't get it out no matter what she tried.

Estelle suggested adding physical activity to her routine, and Luke took her to the gym Mya used to train vampires and teach the women they'd rescued self-defense. The moment Johanna saw Mya fight, she knew this was where she needed to be. Mya agreed to train her, and she was brutal. She didn't hold back punches, she went for the jugular. She was more like a wild tiger than a vampire as she fought, but it was good for Johanna. It fulfilled her need to be useful, to feel strong and capable, while also giving her a place to direct her anger. Over time, Johanna realized that was what Mya used it for as well.

But the anger was still there. It may not have been as loud or as prevalent, but it was there, under everything, in her sinews and bones. It sat in wait until she could use it, and Johanna knew the moment she did she would never be the same.

———

"Show me what Mya's been teaching you," Luke said as he stepped out of their house and into the backyard.

Johanna rotated her elbows and took in his appearance, letting her gaze roam over him. It had been two months since the last time they had been intimate with one another, and even though she knew it was out of consideration for what she'd been through, her desire for him was driving her crazy.

She missed him, and seeing him like this—shirtless, glistening in sweat, his hair pushed back from his forehead from the amount of times he'd raked his gloved hands through it—didn't help. In fact, she wanted to follow the droplets of sweat over his body until—

Johanna ducked as his hand shot out to hit her. She blocked his next strike, then parried with a kick toward his abdomen. He jumped away from her and she planted her hands on her hips.

"What in the hell do you think you're doing?"

"Training ... or trying to. You were too busy staring." He smirked.

"Fine, have it your way."

Johanna launched herself at him. She punched at his chest, and he spun away from her. Luke kicked at her feet, so she jumped away from him. On and on they moved, blocking and countering each other's attacks. As she ducked under another punch, she realized that she was smiling. For the first time in what felt like several grueling weeks, she was having fun.

But then something ran across her body, like a featherlight touch had caressed every inch of her skin all at once, stimulating all of her. She froze, her back arched as a gasp left her, and then Luke swept her feet out from under her and she toppled to the ground.

Johanna tried to get her feet around him in a defensive maneuver, but he seemed to know what she was thinking. He pinned her leg beneath him while pulling the other one over his shoulder. Then he pinned her hands to the sides of her head.

She was breathless, panting from the exertion and from the effect he had on her.

Luke's gaze traveled down her body, then back up. He leaned close to her lips, holding her gaze as he whispered, "I win."

She tried to pull her arms out from his grasp, but he only tightened his grip and held her still. "That was a dirty trick," she said.

"Dirty or not, it got me exactly what I wanted." Luke leaned down to her neck and breathed in. The sigh he released was euphoric as it flitted over her skin, raising goosebumps over her flesh.

"And what is it that you want?"

"Just a kiss," Luke said as he lowered her thigh, fitting himself between her legs.

"Just one?" Johanna whimpered.

Luke smiled. "Unless you're feeling generous."

Johanna licked her lips as she focused on his mouth. She could nearly taste him as she whispered, "Yes. *Always.*"

Luke's lips descended upon hers, but it wasn't the kind of kiss she was used to from him. Her fierce protector had turned soft, gentle, kind, and somehow this simple kiss cut her more than anything else. It opened her to an entirely new universe, where she was the sun and the stars and he was the space that kept her afloat. Without him, without his grasp on her wrists and his gentle fingers on her cheek, his lips would have carried her away. They were so soothing, his kiss so tender, that they unleashed a deep yearning within her soul.

But then he pulled away, just barely. His breath fanned her face, and when she looked into his eyes all she saw was adoration, a love that renewed the strings of her heart and tied her back into him in an infinite loop.

"I love you," he whispered, the words stealing away her breath before he claimed her lips once more.

His fingers tangled with hers as he kept her pinned to the ground with his body. He was overwhelming her senses and yet she couldn't get enough. She couldn't go a second without him knowing, *feeling* what was in her heart for him.

Johanna reopened the telepathic connection between them. She felt his warmth and his love swim through her mind, and she sent hers out to him. She knew the moment he felt it. He shuddered and his lips broke away from hers on a sigh, so she took the chance to whisper back to him, "I love you too. I always will."

The smile he gave her could light up cities, could rival the sun, and in that moment she knew that she would have gone through every second of her life, every horror, again, as long as it lead her to him.

––––––––

It had only become worse. Every moment she spent around Luke was torturous. Johanna couldn't focus during their meditations or when he pulled her onto his lap while they talked. She'd started taking painting lessons from him, yet even those quiet moments where she was supposed to be focusing on her feelings and her art were ruined, all because he wasn't inside her.

Their training sessions—if she could even call them that anymore—were a mess. The amount of times she'd lost now was honestly embarrassing, but it truly wasn't her fault. Luke started teaching her jujutsu, specifically the holds, throws, and various stretches to increase her flexibility. This also meant she spent the majority of her time pressed against him in some way, shape, or form, or on her back with him on top of her.

Perhaps the worst thing of all was how he didn't seem to be affected in the same way she was. He just smiled, or otherwise seemed indifferent when they touched. His mind didn't reveal anything to her either. In fact, he seemed to be distracted, thinking of twenty million things when she was around.

She couldn't make sense of it at all. Did he not feel drawn to her anymore? Did he not desire her, crave her in the same way she did him? Had their connection somehow dulled for him over time? He loved her, but he wouldn't touch her. He was there for her, but he was also miles away. It was maddening. It was heartbreaking. It *hurt.*

Johanna tried to put it behind her. She was just over-reacting. If it wasn't that, then she was sure Luke was somehow doing this for her. He loved her, she knew that. There was not a doubt in her mind when it came to his heart, which meant there had to be an answer somewhere else.

She spoke to Estelle about it, and the therapist's advice was two-fold: To finally be honest with Luke about her desires, something they had been discussing for the last two weeks, and to just ask him. But Johanna couldn't. She tried to tell herself it was because she valued Luke's wishes and trusted his choices. And she did. Johanna believed in Luke truly, but a small seed of doubt was beginning to grow in her, and without any reassurance it was taking root. The roots steadied, grew, and then one day bore fruit.

Johanna heard the shower running with her enhanced senses, but after a while she picked up on another sound. It was small, muffled by the water, but it was there. She stepped closer to the room, then past the bed, and she realized what it was.

A moan.

Luke was in there. It was his voice, his moans that filled the room. Johanna was shocked, broken as she stood there listening to the man she loved get off on something that wasn't her. Her feet moved unconsciously, heart crumbling with every step she took and with every note of his pleasure. She didn't realize what she was doing until she slammed the bathroom door open.

Luke whirled around, wide eyed, his hand still around his cock, and betrayal surged through her that he would rather do this than be inside of her.

"Sunflower—"

She shook her head, backing away as he began to exit the shower. He took a step toward her, so she ran. Johanna didn't know what she was doing or where she was going, but hearing his footsteps behind her made her legs move faster. Johanna used every bit of her vampire speed to get away from him, because she couldn't be around him right now. She couldn't bear to see the evidence that she had tried to fight against. He didn't desire her, not anymore. But could she blame him after she'd been ruined by his enemy, after the last few months of her healing and trauma? It was too much for him.

That was the last thought she had before she went flying through the air.

Luke turned, cradling her as they landed and taking the force of the impact. She tried to sit up to get off and away from him, but he rolled them over and pinned her down. Johanna struggled against him, trying to push, pull, buck him off her until—

"Stop!"

His voice quelled her fight. The dark growl commanded her to listen, to obey, and she hated her treacherous body for it. Tears of frustration clouded her eyes, but she shook her head to clear them. She was ready to give him a piece of her mind, but she froze the moment she saw the bright red glow in his eyes.

"Johanna, why the fuck did you run from me?"

"You know why!" She tried to pull out of his grip again, but he only tightened his clasp on her wrists, squeezing until she whimpered.

"No. If I knew why, I wouldn't be asking. Why were you running? What triggered your blood lust? Tell me, right now."

Her eyes widened as she realized they must be just as red as his were. She tilted her head away, shame flowing through her, but he grasped her chin hard and pulled her back to meet his gaze.

"*Now*," he growled.

"You!" Tears pooled in her eyes. She blinked them away, but her voice still quivered as she spoke. "You don't want me anymore."

"Why would you—" Luke ran a hand through his hair and let out a frustrated sigh. "For the love of the gods. Baby, *of course* I want you."

"Then why won't you take me?" she yelled.

"That's what this is about?" He breathed, and then his lips twitched into that damn frustrating smirk and she saw red.

"Yes!" Johanna swore that somehow his eyes burned brighter at her outburst, but that didn't stop her. "We haven't been intimate in months! You sit here and do these training sessions with me, where you do nothing but tease me every damn second, but you're not affected by them, by *me*. Being close to me does nothing to you! Instead, you wear the same fucking smile you have on your face right now! And then, to make matters worse, I find you jerking off in the shower. You'd rather do that than be inside of me, and it *hurts!*"

"Sunflower—"

"Don't fucking call me that!"

Suddenly Luke's fingers wrapped around her throat. He squeezed and the sensation went straight to her core. Her lips parted and he loosened his grip enough to let her pull in a breath.

"Now are you going to be a good girl and let me speak, or do I need to find other ways to keep you quiet?"

She moaned. Gods help her, she moaned. "Luke—"

He growled in response and lowered his head to hers until he was all she could see, all she could feel, until he overwhelmed her senses in just the way she longed for him to. "You don't speak. You don't say a single word until I finish. Do you understand?"

Goosebumps broke out over her skin from the danger in his voice, the very threat of punishment if she didn't comply. She licked her lips and his eyes fell there for a moment before he shuddered, his fingers flexing around her throat, choking her once more. The look in his eyes, his wildness, his pleasure, had her spreading her legs wider for him. He pushed against her pelvis and it was only then that she realized he was fully naked and still incredibly hard.

He took her silence as her answer, and his fingers ran over her skin. "Everything you said was wrong."

She opened her mouth to argue but his sharp look practically *dared* her to disobey him. She promptly pressed her lips back together.

"I started those training sessions for two reasons. One was to help you. Really, it was, but the other reason was much more selfish."

His hand ran down her shirt and he ripped it away from her. His aggression made her cry out as the walls of her pussy clenched, already wet and begging for him to fill her.

Luke's eyes ran over her breasts, still in her bra, and then he ripped it away from her too. He tore it into shreds as if the material had offended him somehow. "You drive me crazy, sunflower. Absolutely crazy, and I needed another way to get my hands on you while still understanding you may need time to heal."

His hands drifted lower over her stomach. She arched her back, her skin heated by his touch. He groaned as he ripped away the closure of her pants, tore at them until there was nothing left.

"You said my teasing hurt you, well it fucking *killed* me, but I hoped it would help to make you comfortable with me, and that eventually you'd desire my touch again. What I didn't know was that somehow I'd make you lose your damn mind and think I didn't want you." Luke brushed the tip of his dick in between her folds and they both moaned. "Does that feel like I don't want you?"

She whimpered, wanting to answer but not wanting to break his rule.

A dark chuckle rumbled through him. "You can answer that," he said, leaning down and sucking her neck, making her moan again.

Johanna arched against him, lifted her hips, and tried to get him inside of her, but he moved so slowly, so calculated and controlled that she wanted to scream. She was so far gone she whimpered, barely able to speak. "N-no. But the shower."

Luke gripped her hips, keeping her still. "I love you. I love you enough to try to be gentle with you, to be vulnerable with you. All those times you were underneath me I wanted to rut you like a damn dog in heat. I imagined I could damn near feel your pussy swallowing me whole. But you needed time. I needed you. I still need you and I still want you. I want you so much it hurts."

He brushed her hair away from her face, the action completely at odds with the crazed look in his eyes. "What you saw in the shower was that. I needed to be inside of you so badly that it fucking hurt, and I thought, stupidly, that maybe I could take care of it, and that once I did it would be better for the both of us. I was barely hanging on, and while I knew you'd let me fuck you, I didn't want you to regret it." His grip on her wrists tightened. "But I couldn't come."

Her eyes widened but he continued.

"That's right, I can't come if I'm not inside of you. I can't come if the scent of you isn't on me, if your pussy isn't sucking me dry."

Johanna moaned his name. She writhed underneath him, so close to coming from his words alone that she knew she'd explode the moment he entered her.

"It's the same thing for you too, isn't it, sunflower?" His fingertips grazed her clit and she arched under him as if struck by lightning. "You can't come if it isn't with me. Say it."

"Yes!" she cried.

"Good girl," he purred as he pinched her clit. "Now

tell me you want it. Tell me you want my cock inside your drenched pussy. I need to hear it before I take you."

The words were on the tip of her lips, but she swallowed them back, needing to say something else instead. "Luke, let go of my wrists, please."

"Are you going to try to hit me?"

She shook her head and he let them go. Johanna brought her hands to his face, cupping her cheeks. "I've been practicing how to say this to you."

His eyes widened. "Practicing?"

She nodded, then she licked her lips, took a deep breath, and gazed into his blood red eyes. "I want you to come inside of me, Luke. Please, be rough with me."

Luke cursed, his whole body shuddering against hers. Then with a groan he thrust inside of her, filling her to the brim.

Johanna wrapped her arms and legs around him as her orgasm rolled through her. Luke's hands went into her hair, pulling her head back as he sunk his fangs into her neck, tilted her hips, then reached his own climax inside of her. But they both needed more.

Luke's cock never softened. Instead, Johanna swore it grew harder as he rammed inside of her. Her moans filled the air, carried off by the wind as she went wild beneath him. Johanna scored his back with her nails, digging them into his flesh as he pounded inside of her.

Luke lifted his head and offered his neck to her. When her fangs slid into his skin, she swore she reached a new level of euphoria. He moaned her name, squeezed her hips and fucked the ever-loving shit out of her. He never stopped, never slowed, not even when they both came again.

Before Johanna knew what was happening, she was on her stomach. "Knees up," was all Luke said, and she instantly did as she was told.

His fingers slid through her pussy lips, and she looked back in time to see the utter look of pleasure on his face, even as she felt it radiate through her body.

"This is how I like to see you, fucking dripping in my come."

"Yes!" she cried as he slid two fingers inside of her, making them both moan.

He took his fingers out and she clenched around him, trying to keep them inside of her. The action made him chuckle, even as he lined himself up with her. "You want me that bad, hmm?"

"Yes," she purred.

Luke cursed and held the fingers that were just inside of her to her lips.

"Suck," he said.

She obeyed, making him curse again. Then he slipped his fingers out of her mouth and rammed his cock inside her pussy in one full thrust. They both gasped. Luke leaned down over her body, pushing her further into the dirt. He gathered her hair in his hand, twisting it around his fist.

"This is for you telling me not to call you my sunflower. That is *my* name for you, and if you ever tell me not to call you that again I will make sure my handprint stays on your ass *permanently.*"

She looked back at him with a smirk of her very own and said, "Yes, sir."

Luke's eyes fell shut. He trembled against her, and she felt every bit of the pleasure that word had caused him. Then he pulled out of her and rammed back inside so hard she nearly lost her balance. "Fucking brat."

"Yours," she said in a moan as he moved again.

"Yes, always mine" he hissed. There was no more room for words as he took her, his hand on her shoulder and her hair wrapped in his fist.

He fucked her as if he was a starved, crazed man, and Johanna was right there with him. Then Luke used his powers. Shadows wrapped around her, and she felt as if a thousand fingertips were caressing her body, squeezing her breasts, clamping down on her nipples, teasing her clit, grabbing her ass. Unable to take the stimulation, she shouted his name into the forest just as he roared hers as he came. Then he pulled her back onto her knees, his hand wrapped around her throat as he bucked inside of her. She laid her hand over his and squeezed. He groaned, tilted his head to the side and sank his fangs back into her skin.

Johanna's hips moved of their own accord. He fucked her and she rode him as they both worked themselves in a frenzy, nearing another explosive orgasm.

Luke offered her his arm, so she bit into it, drinking his blood, letting it fill her and take her over completely just as the rest of him had. She was his and he was hers, and as they mated in the forest she swore they both screamed loud enough that the whole world heard it.

CHAPTER 19

Johanna smiled as the sunlight caught on the teardrop diamond engagement ring on her finger. She spread her fingers around the steering wheel, admiring how the light hit the gem at different angles.

Luke and Johanna were doing well. They'd learned to stop keeping secrets from one another, no matter how embarrassing or insecure it might make them, and it made a world of a difference. The night of Greg and Dani's wedding, Luke pulled her aside and finally told her that he'd searched for and found her family. She was overjoyed that he'd done this for her, but even more so when he explained that he wanted ask them for her hand in marriage. Johanna said yes, even though he refused to accept her answer until he received their blessing.

Their first meeting hadn't exactly been ideal. Her family was wary of Luke after they found out everything that happened to her, even though their connection and mate bond were obvious. Still, he wore them down until he got their blessing, and now they were discussing dates for their own wedding.

Johanna caught her reflection in the window. Her blue eyes shone, her skin glowed and she knew it was all because of him. Her Luke. She was so happy, so at peace in the serenity that he'd wrapped her in. He'd taught her so much about love, about life, and he made her excited for every day she saw, all because she knew he would be right there beside her. She never knew things could be so good, never imagined her life could be so filled with joy, and she was grateful for it all. In fact, she couldn't wait to get home and show that gratefulness to him.

Johanna turned down the road to their house, but instead of bliss, she only felt dread. She wasn't sure why. She knew Luke was home and waiting for her, yet something just felt off. Johanna tried to reach him telepathically, but she couldn't. There was only static, as if their connection had been severed.

That was impossible. While Johanna had taught Luke ways to shield his mind, he didn't have the ability to shield her, nor would he want to. This wasn't like him. Something was wrong.

Johanna threw the car in park and bounded up the stairs. She went to grab the handle of the front door but paused. Luke and Mya had trained her for things like this. She couldn't just go barging in. She needed to be logical first and push her emotions to the side.

She took a deep breath. Johanna couldn't smell anyone else outside, nor could she see anyone, but she could feel something or someone trying to mask their energy, and it wasn't Luke.

Johanna opened the door to their house. She let the mate bond pull her to Luke, but as she got closer, she heard a laugh, a voice that chilled her to the bone.

No.

Her eyes locked on Luke when she stepped inside the room, but his expression was blank as he stared at her. Beside him she saw the one man she hoped to never see alive again.

Zachariah.

"Hello, pet."

That word triggered such an adverse reaction in her that she nearly vomited on the spot. Instead, Johanna swallowed back the bile and stood taller. She would not let him get to her. She would not be a pawn in his games ever again. "What do you want, Zachariah?"

"That answer should be obvious. You."

Johanna laughed, cackled at the fucking audacity of this godforsaken creature. "I'm not sure what level of delusion you're on that makes you believe that's ever going to happen, but the answer is no."

"Aw, pet." He held his hands out to her, an evil grin on his face. "Didn't you miss me? We did such great things together. You were a beautiful weapon, and since you had such a hard time staying away from your mate, I even brought him over to our side just for you. You're welcome," he spat.

Johanna didn't have to ask what he'd done to Luke. It was obvious in the blood that marred his skin, in the way he didn't move, barely even blinked when his nemesis stood beside him.

"Cat got your tongue? That's alright. Today's a celebration day for me so I'm willing to let impudence slide. But here's the thing, either you come with me, or I'll just find someone else." He grinned. "Like your little sister, Tamara, or maybe your mother, Corrine."

Her eyes widened at their names.

"That's right. Luke tried not to give me the information, but in the end he was just too weak." Zachariah shrugged. "Your choice of mate was honestly abysmal, Johanna."

"Fine, I'll go," she said with a nod, a plan forming in her mind.

Zachariah smiled. "I knew I could count on you to make the right choice."

She smiled back, feeling her grin grow. The rage that had been dormant within her came to the surface, and with it her powers. Johanna pushed past the magic Constance used to guard Zachariah, and dove into his mind. It was a place of nightmares and terror, covered in so much tar and darkness that she doubted anyone could stay unscathed for long. But that didn't matter, because now that she had wormed her way inside, she could read him like a book.

Luke moved under Zachariah's silent command. He lunged at her clumsily, a by-product of Constance's possession, but Luke had trained her how to protect herself from anyone, including him. She grabbed hold of his arm and ducked, spinning underneath him. The momentum made him flip over her and crash to the floor. Instantaneously, she pulled out of Zachariah's mind and into Luke's, issuing a command to force him to sleep.

Zachariah appeared in front of her in a flash, a smile on his face as if he'd won his prize. She wasn't surprised to find him crowding her space, nor was she fearful when he grabbed her. Instead, she let him.

"It's cute that you thought that would work," he said with a sneer.

She smirked. "Oh, I didn't. I just needed to separate the two of you."

"And what did you think that would achieve?"

"This."

She spun. Using her momentum, she turned her hand to the side and struck his neck, directly on his carotid artery. His eyes grew wide as he staggered back from her, and it only served to make her smile larger.

"You see, I know your powers enhance your body, but that enhancement is triggered by your mind. Without that trigger, well, you're just an old, weak sack of shit."

"What did you do?" he screeched.

"Simply switched your power off. I'm giving you a dose of your own medicine, Zachariah. It hurts, doesn't it, to feel less than."

She kicked him in the ribs.

"To feel powerless."

She kicked him again.

"To have your abilities, the very essence of who you are, taken from you."

Zachariah reared back to punch her, but she spun, dodging the attack only to kick him in the face and smile triumphantly as he went down.

"This is impossible," he bit out. "There's no way you could be stronger than me."

She smiled and let him get up before she looked him dead in his eyes. "I've always been stronger than you. A fucking ant is stronger than you. You just had opportunity and a sick, perverse agenda funded by an absolute bitch. Your only strengths were your powers and your ability to hold things over another person's head. Without those you're *nothing*. And the moment, the fucking *second* you touched my mate, you were never going to make it out of here alive."

He roared and moved to attack her, but Johanna was quicker, freezing his body in place.

The windows shattered and the doors slammed open as twenty of Zachariah's men invaded the house.

"Am I supposed to be scared?" Johanna said. They tried to move, but she froze them in place as well.

"When you started losing, you stopped focusing on whatever magic it was that let you mask your group. But now that the gangs all here, I think it's time to say goodbye."

Johanna dug deep inside of herself, pouring everything she could into her attack, every ounce of rage, betrayal, and hurt fueled her power. She raised her hands to the ceiling as the men struggled to break free of her magic, but she wouldn't let them. She looked at Luke's sleeping form one more time before she slammed her hands down to her sides.

Her power surged through the house, and then the building caved in on itself. Every inch of the roof and every section of every floor imploded and crashed down upon Zachariah and the men he'd brought with him.

Johanna staggered under her magic, but she refused to fall. Her job wasn't done yet.

She reached for the dagger Luke forced her to carry, and went to the last place she'd seen Zachariah. Using her magic, she lifted the heavy stone and concrete to reveal his crushed form. Even though she believed he was dead, she had to make sure. She pushed the knife through his flesh, skull, and into his brain, but only when she pulled it out was she satisfied.

Then she fell. Weak and tired, she crawled over to Luke and pulled him into her arms. The battle may have been over, but the one inside of him was still raging strong. Johanna was sure that when he came to, he would still be under the effects of Constance's possession magic, and there was only one thing she thought could break it.

Using the last ounces of her strength, Johanna teleported them both to Dani and Greg's house. She struggled to breathe, the exertion of her powers taking over, but still she fought her unconsciousness. She had to take care of Luke. He had to be okay.

They crash-landed in the kitchen.

"What the fuck?" Dani yelled as she sprung up from her seat, cradling her bump.

"Johanna, what happened?" Greg asked.

"It was Zachariah." Johanna looked around. "Where's Mya?"

"Mya? Wait. What do you mean Zachariah? Johanna, what the fuck happened?" Dani said.

"We don't have time! Please, I think Mya can help me get him back to normal. Where is she?"

Greg already had her on the line. "She's getting here as fast as she can."

"How long?" Johanna asked, running her hand over Luke's cheek.

"Twenty minutes," Greg said.

"Tell her to hurry, please. I don't know how much longer I can stay conscious." Johanna groaned. The feedback from the amount of power she used hit her all at once and she screamed as pain flew through her.

Dani held onto her as she swayed. "Johanna!"

"I'm fine. I'll be fine. I just used too much power."

Greg came to her side. "What can we do to help you?"

"Nothing." She looked up at him. "Zachariah must have ambushed Luke at our house. They gave him Constance's blood and he's under her possession magic. I forced him to sleep, but the last command Zachariah gave him was to hurt me. If I fall unconscious, it's the first thing he'll do."

"How do we get him out of it?" Dani asked.

"Blood. I'm going to try to force my powers into him through my blood. I think if we mix that with Mya's then it will sever the magic."

Dani immediately grabbed a bowl and knife to collect Johanna's blood.

"Johanna, where is Zachariah?" Greg asked.

"Dead."

Dani whirled back around to her as Greg's eyes widened.

"I killed him. Him and twenty of his men," she said through the pain. She ran her hand through Luke's hair. "He won't be able to hurt anyone else."

"Are you sure he's dead?" Greg asked.

Johanna pulled out the dagger she'd used to stab Zachariah. "I stabbed his brain with this. You'll find his body, as well as the others, underneath the rubble of our house." She swayed again, almost falling to the side, but Greg caught her. "I won't be able to stay conscious for much longer. Take care of him, please."

"Of course," he said.

As her consciousness faded, Johanna whispered, "Tell him … I love … him—"

Then she screamed as pain flooded her body and the world went black.

———

She was warm, so incredibly warm and comfortable. The arm around her waist tightened, and Johanna snuggled further into Luke's chest.

Luke.

Her eyes snapped open. She lifted her head from his neck and stared down at him.

"Luke?"

Please don't be a dream, please don't be a dream.

"Good morning, sunflower," he said with a small smile.

"Luke!" She threw her arms around him, laughing even as she cried.

Luke clung to her, kissing her head and every bit of skin he could find. She joined him, kissing his beard, his jaw, his chin, his lips. She laughed until she felt the wetness from his own eyes on his cheeks. Johanna had never seen him cry, and it broke her heart to do so.

"Baby," she whispered, wiping away the moisture.

He shook his head. "I saw you. The whole time, I saw you standing there with Zachariah next to you and I couldn't reach out to you. I couldn't get to you. I'm so sorry. I'm so, so sorry."

She shook her head as her tears fell and mixed with his own. "No, please no. I know what you went through and I know what it feels like. Please don't blame yourself."

"I have to. I let you down, I was supposed to protect you—"

"You did!" Johanna kissed his hands. "You did. If it wasn't for you, I wouldn't have known how to fight. I wouldn't have found the courage."

He smiled, brushing away her tears. "You were amazing, but you used so much power. You've been asleep for days, sunflower. I was so scared."

"I'm sorry, but I had to make sure you were safe. I didn't want him to ever hurt you, me, or anyone ever again."

He kissed her head as he cradled her to his chest, his grip hard and sure on her body. "You made sure of that."

She nodded, breathing in his scent, but then she pulled back in shock. "What happened when I passed out? Was anyone hurt? Were we able to clear Constance's magic? Did it hurt you?"

"No," he said, but his smile was pained. "Greg tied me down after you lost consciousness. Mixing your blood with Mya's worked to clear the possession. I was back to normal within a few minutes." Luke ran his fingers through her hair. "You saved me, sunflower, my little warrior."

"I swore I would do anything for you, even—"

"Fight, maim, or kill. I remember."

They shared a small smile before Johanna rested her head back in the crook of his neck. "About our house…"

He laughed, the sound vibrating through him so hard it shook her. "Yeah, that's not getting fixed for a while."

She frowned. "I'm sorry."

"Don't be. A house can be repaired or fixed, or a new one bought, but there is nothing in this world that matters more than you."

She kissed his neck, and he ran his palms over her back, kneading her muscles.

"Where do we go from here?" she asked.

"Well, we should probably find another house to buy, and there are a million other things that we'll have to fix to win this war and protect the people we love." His hands slid down to her ass and he squeezed her cheeks. "But for right now, I was thinking that we happen to be safe, alone, and already in bed. It would be a shame to waste such a wonderful opportunity."

She laughed as he rolled them over and settled between her thighs.

"I've missed you," he whispered, kissing her shoulder and sliding down the strap of her nightgown.

She cupped his face and stared deeply into the most beautiful mix of green and gray. "I love you."

Luke's eyes softened, filled with adoration and passion. He cupped her hands and whispered against her lips, "I love you too, and I will for the rest of time."

. . .

The End of book 2, Night Fury: Chronicles of The Otherworld.

———

Continue the series with Night Fall! There's no line Mya and Erik won't cross for one another, and may the gods have mercy on their enemies, because they certainly won't. Turn the page to read the first chapter or use the QR code below and enter discount code: **VAMPIRE-SAVE35** to save 35% off!

Don't forget to join my newsletter to get a bonus scene with Daniella and Johanna, all the latest updates, ARC opportunities, and more.

NIGHT FALL PREVIEW

The first time she met him, she was dying.

The plague had taken over villages, entire continents. So many lives had been lost and now that tally included her mother, father, and aunt. Mya tried to take care of them, tried to hope that if she could just do something, that if she was fast enough, worked hard enough, they would survive. And if not, at least she could help them hold on until her brother, Gregori, came back with a cure. He would come back; she was sure of it. They all just had to stay strong and have faith until then.

But hours turned into days, days into weeks, and still Gregori was gone. And now she, and her cousin, Lucas, had fallen ill.

Waiting for a cure changed to waiting for death. Mya could feel the Black Plague eating away at her flesh, fogging her mind, ruining her, turning her into something other than the young, healthy, vibrant girl she once was.

At the end, there was no one left to watch over them. No one to feed them, wash them, or ease their suffering. Mya and Lucas had tried so hard not to succumb to the illness, but eventually they collapsed on the floor, and soon they were covered in their own boils, piss, vomit, and fecal matter, too weak to move. If the plague did not kill them, starvation would.

It was difficult to know she was dying and could not do a single thing about it. Mya did not want to die, but what was the alternative? Even if Gregori came back with a cure, it would never revive the limbs she lost to gangrene, or the delirium that had set in at her high fever. And who was to say that Gregori was still alive? He may be just as dead as she was bound to be.

That was the state Gregori had found them in. She could not see clearly by the time Gregori and his companion entered their small family home. She half thought she had imagined his return. But then she heard his companion's voice, and it stole her entire focus. Mya did not know what it was about that voice. She had heard men speak before, and while she and Lucas had been alone for some time, she still remembered the voices of the other inhabitants of their village ... back when they were still alive, that was. Still, the slightly accented voice—so deep and rich, patient and controlled, yet strained, as if he cared about her survival—touched her, deeply. That there was anyone left to care when she was so close to death warmed her heart, made her suffering ease just slightly.

It was a mixture of that feeling and the panic in Gregori's voice that made tears spill from her eyes. It was too late. She was too far gone, and she wished her brother had been saved from seeing her like this so that he could remember her the way she was before the plague, before he left. Yet her single string of happiness came from the notion that he would be by her side when she died.

Her wish to have him near her was a selfish one. She looked up to him, respected him, wanted more for him, but also needed him. He gave her the courage she needed to accept her death without bitterness or resentment.

But then she felt his presence next to her. He was far too close. And what about Lucas? Why was Gregori not going to Lucas? Had he already died? Was she the only one left, deliriously waiting for hope when there was none?

No, there may not be hope for her, and perhaps there was no hope for her cousin, but Gregori should survive. He *needed* to survive, which meant he needed to leave this plague infested house and save himself.

Gregori moved to cradle her, but she pushed him away. He leaned over her once more, and she fought with all her might to shove him once again. That bought her a few inches, but she was too weak for anything more.

Gregori warned her not to fight him, but still she thrashed. She sobbed in their native tongue, warning him, *begging* him to save Lucas, and if he could not, to at least save himself.

Then a hand, heavy but gentle, grasped her shoulder, surging warmth through her body. Mya's blurry eyes shifted to Gregori's companion's as the man spoke for the first time, "Be still. Gregori has brought you a cure. Listen to your brother and take it."

The last of her energy fled from her as if it had been washed away by a great tide, and she fell back onto the hard floor, so tired that she could do nothing more but obey. The stranger touched her again, his hand shifting to her jaw where he squeezed until he forced her to open her cracked and bleeding lips.

Liquid dripped into her mouth and slid to the back of her throat. She swallowed, and the first wave of heat hit her, pleasurable and shocking. Mya could suddenly taste a fury of flavors—acidic, meaty, savory, salty, iron, and something almost close to smoke. Every part of her being came alive as fire burst through her body, setting her aflame. She felt renewed, energized, capable, stronger than she had ever been in her entire life. She wanted more of the delicious drink; she *craved* it.

Unable to control her fervor and now free from the stranger's touch, she grasped her brother's hand to her lips and sunk her teeth—no, no longer teeth ... *fangs*—into Gregori's wrist, drinking his blood in mouthfuls. She should have been disgusted by the notion, concerned by her illness, but she was too lost to the power he had given her through his blood. It was only when the stranger pulled her away, did she settle calmly onto her back, high on something she could not name.

She felt her brother leave her and move to the side where she had last seen her cousin. After several moments, her eyes focused and she glanced at the unknown being in front of her. A gasp left her lips at his beauty, and she blushed at the twitch of a smile on his lips, embarrassed by her state of undress and filth.

That was the first time she met Erik Devereux, and he looked like an angel.

———

Scan the QR code below to continue reading now!

ABOUT THE AUTHOR

Melissa had a difficult time speaking as a child, and thus writing became her best friend. There she learned the power of emotion, how to communicate heartbreak, sadness, tragedy, and still hope for something better: the happy ever after.

She loves to write imperfect, possessive heroes, that will risk their lives for those they love, strong heroines that can hold their own, and steamy scenes that grab you by the throat and bring you to your knees.

Melissa lives in a small town off the coast of Egypt, and is a huge mythology buff, with a love of all things magical, supernatural, paranormal, and steeped in lore and fantasy. When she is not writing Melissa can be found singing and dancing her heart out, or up, late at night, contemplating space and the universe with a large cup of tea.

facebook.com/MelissaCumminsAuthor

instagram.com/melissacumminsauthor

bookbub.com/profile/melissa-cummins

ACKNOWLEDGMENTS

To my editor, Ellen, thank you so much for all you've done. You are always such a joy to work with and you really add the extra shine into my work. It wouldn't be the same without you.

To Emily, thank you for all of your feedback and suggestions!

Taylor, your feedback made me laugh out loud. Thank you for helping me calm my nerves about so many little tidbits and being such a wonderful friend.

To Sarah, Paige, and Dee, thank you both for all of your support and just being so wonderful!

To you. Yes! You! Thank you so much for reading my novel. Knowing that you took the the time to read it is beyond amazing to me. You help every author to move forward, to write their next book, to publish, to celebrate. That's all you. So thank you again, take care, and I can't wait for you to read my next book!